MW01126404

BLACKSTONE

A FOUR FATHERS STORY

Lily ♡
ENJOY Naughty Trevor!
♡ JDH

J.D. HOLLYFIELD

I am meticulous. Structured. A single father.

I obsess over things and crave control.
And when a hot, feisty little woman throws a wrench in my carefully laid out plans, I lose my mind.
My every thought revolves around making her bend to my will—until they become less about her doing things my way and more about just her.

My name is Trevor Blackstone.

I am an obsessive, complicated, demanding man.
People may not understand me, but it doesn't stop them from wanting me.

DEDICATION

I dedicate this book to red wine.
You really know how to bring the words out of me.

ONE

TREVOR

"JUST ANOTHER FUCKED UP DAY IN PARADISE,"
I mumble, walking out of my lavish eighty-
two hundred square foot beachfront palace overlooking
the crystal-clear beaches of the Tampa Bay shores. The
sarcasm of my statement dripping with bullshit as I jump
into my Aston Martin One-77 and speed off. Weaving
through the sunny Florida rush hour traffic, I manage
to avoid hitting a pedestrian chasing after a dog running
across the street. It wasn't just luck, though. It's because
numbers are my thing. My brain is fucked up. Constant
numbers, calculations. Formation of fractions, equations.
Shit, I can go on and on. Science of patterns. My brain
never sleeps.

Math is in fucking everything. Orderliness, balance,

logic—all the shit I need to do my job. All the mental traits it takes to live.

Therefore, when my brain doesn't sleep, I don't sleep.

Picture that cartoon figure walking with the constant bubble above his head figuring out equations. Got it? That's me. Math prodigy.

I pull into the underground parking lot of my company, Four Fathers Freight, and park in my reserved spot. The one that says Owner. I'm tempted to have maintenance change it to *Motherfuckin'* Owner, because when you're the boss, you can do whatever the fuck you want. But I'm just one of four—four powerful men who created an empire.

I jump out of my car, grab for my phone, and lock her. Yeah, she's a her. Because she purrs like a kitten in heat when I get her up to a hundred in less than sixty seconds. I wish some of the women I brought home purred as nice as she did. That thought reminds me of one of three voicemails I have sitting on my phone. Some of many fires I have to put out today.

Entering the private entrance, I press my open palm up to the scanner, accessing the elevator designed just for the seventieth floor. When the ding notifies me the ride's over, it opens just in time for me to witness the usual fucked up shit I try to avoid.

"Morning," I grumble as Levi Kingston, one of the partners, makes a half ass effort to pull himself away from our receptionist without bothering to remove his hand from her thigh.

Of course, the asshole just smiles at me. "Ahhh, in early I see," he says, bringing his predatorial eyes back to the girl, not caring he just got caught breaking a shit ton of employment regulations. Not that everyone else in this fucking company doesn't break rules. It seems as if I'm the only levelheaded one around here when it comes to women. Simply because I stay the fuck away from them.

A reminder of the second message sitting on my phone I have to deal with.

I step forward, allowing the receptionist to hand me

the mail. "Good morning, Mr. Blackstone. I forwarded all the calls that came in over the weekend to your personal line," she stutters, her nerves getting the best of her. Good to know she at least realizes fraternizing with her boss is frowned upon in the workforce.

"Trev, we were just discussing a company team builder. What do you say, a work party at one of your beachfront properties?" I look at Levi, surprised he's even sitting on her desk. I haven't seen a wrinkle in his top-of-the-line suit since the day I met him. Two hundred and twelve seconds have passed since I've walked into the office, and with the tilt of his lean, add on the abrasion to the fabric, he's creating seven creases in his pants, three in his suit coat, and one in my forehead at the lawsuit when our admin learns all the heavy shit he's into and screams assault.

"I'll have to check to see what's available. Got work to do." Waving them off, I head to my office, shut the door, and throw myself into my leather chair. With a swift twist, I face toward the wall of glass windows and stare out into the water.

I love the fucking water.

It's why I moved to Tampa. Why I forced Eric Pearson, my best friend and partner, to start up Four Fathers here and not in New York. I handle all numbers for the company. I've handled them since back in college when starting Four Fathers was just an idea Eric and I conjured up one night while drinking expensive bourbon his father sent for him passing yet another class with flying colors. Little does his rich asshole father know, it was me taking those tests.

I watch a few surfers hit the water, wishing I was on the other side of the glass not dealing with bullshit at work, when my phone alerts me to a new voicemail. Looking at the missed number, a small sigh of relief floods through me. One good thing: my realtor. Hopefully she locked down the last property on Flanders Bay—the last house on the mile-long oceanfront subdivision I don't own.

First things first, I listen to the voicemail that's been

sitting in my inbox since late last night. I know this isn't gonna be pretty. I press play, and close my eyes, waiting for the bitching to begin.

"Trevor, this is Susan. You know, the one you blew off tonight, you fucking prick! I waited for almost three hours for you. Hope you choke on your own dick, loser!"

Pretty much what I expected to hear. Maybe I should call her back and tell her she should update her fucking photo on her dating site so her future dates know she looks more like a cow than a high school varsity cheerleader. Christ. Then, when I got to the restaurant last night after unwillingly being set up by my ex, perhaps I wouldn't have walked right out after seeing what a hot mess she was. I don't know what it is with women and Botox nowadays. The sight of her lips didn't turn me on. They fucking scared me. The image of her suffocating my poor cock with those gigantic things had me turning around and running south.

This leads me to the second voicemail. The call I missed this morning from Darlene, my ex. I wish that bitch would stop meddling in my life by trying to set me up on blind dates with women who look like lab experiments. I take a deep breath and hit play.

"Trevor, what the fuck? I just got off the phone with Susan and she told me you blew her off last night! She's a great gal. Gives great head, from what I hear. You need to start dating, Trev. It's not good for our son to see you always so closed off. Bringing home random girls doesn't set a good example for him. Anyway, call her. I think she'd be willing to reschedule. Kiki and I give our love. See you Sunday!"

My dick and I both say no thank you to the reschedule. And Kaden, our son, is almost twenty-one and away at college. He's old enough to mind his own business. If anyone should be worried about our son, it's her and the way she swapped for the other team.

Yeah, that's right. Darlene, after twenty-one years of marriage, went through a midlife crisis, took off to Vegas one day, and came home weeks later in love with a stripper. *Female* stripper. I thought it was just a phase. I let her ride it out—or ride out the chick twenty years

younger she was experimenting with. I told myself I
would back off while she snapped out of it. I was always
so damn busy with work, I could understand. She was
just lonely. Needed the affection. I was glad it wasn't
another dude. It was actually hot, I thought. But then, one
night, I was drunk as a skunk and came home to them on
the couch eating each other out like fucking carnivores.
Tried to get in the middle of that, and her lover punched
me in the dick while Darlene just cried, telling me she
wanted a divorce.

So, while I ended up with a really sore dick and blue
balls, they ended up with my house, alimony, and partial
custody of our son.

It's been five years, so my balls have recovered, but
I'm not sure my dick has. When your wife leaves you for
a woman, you start to wonder what was so wrong with
the big guy in the first place. I wasn't a cheater or a beater.
I didn't verbally abuse her or step out on her. I may have
been absent for a lot of our marriage, but that's what
came with being on top. I worked twenty-four hours a

day, and she wanted for nothing. Well, apparently, what she wanted was more pussy in her life.

I delete the message knowing I'm not going to call her back. She'll have enough to say on Sunday when she comes over with the newest design layout for staging the Flanders property, which is soon to be torn down and built into a luxurious mansion, set to match the rest of the houses on the beach.

Don't let that statement confuse you. Darlene doesn't work for me. She didn't work a single day we were married, and damn if she thought to get a job after we divorced. She gave me some, *"What would our son think to see his poor mother suffering in the workforce?"* sob story bullshit. I told her he would see a woman earning her keep like everyone else in the fucking world. That also fell on deaf ears. Instead, she spends my money like it's her fucking job, purchasing anything and everything as if the sky's the limit. I'm pretty sure I just funded her girlfriend's new boob job. Luckily for me, part of that spending entails buying shit to furnish and decorate each house I purchase—a task I want nothing to do with.

The first two messages have me pulling out my desk drawer and reaching for my Tums. It's not even nine in the morning and I'm already calculating the minutes it's gonna take for these fuckers to dissolve and not fix the stress burn in my stomach. I have a ton of meetings and Eric will be in soon wanting to work the numbers on the new warehouse going up in south Miami.

I decide to avoid the third voicemail and listen to the one that just came through.

"Trevor, Clara Hill. It seems we ran into a bit of a problem with the sale of 1543 Flanders Bay. The owner's granddaughter is holding the sale 'til the end of the summer. She refuses, even for a higher bid, to sign off on the contract until then, claiming she's staying at the residence. Let me know how you want us to proceed."

"Son of a bitch." The one call that was supposed to bring some joy to my day. "Fuck!" I've been working on the sale of that house for months. The property next door is a shack and in desperate need of a renovation. As in, tear the ugly fucker down and rebuild to match the other houses on the block. When I bought my house, there was nobody living in it. Probably due to the condition of it.

I got the call a few months ago from my realtor saying the woman who owned it was finally ready to sell. My team was pushing for a quick sale, and I was willing to pay way over what it was worth. The shit thing is, she died before I got that damn amendment signed, which left our deal in the hands of her executor of trust—her granddaughter. The end of the summer wasn't gonna work for me. That woman was signing off on that sale—and now.

I text Clara telling her to handle it and not call back until she has an agreement. I want the closing date to be yesterday. It's rare anyone tells me no, hence why I have the entire construction set for three days from today. What I don't need is their little granddaughter trying to work more money out of me and stall my plans.

The anxiety of how this setback will domino effect the rest of the project sends my mind into overdrive.

Dropping my phone, I bring my fingers to my temples and press hard enough to bruise. I do as Dr. Winters taught me and begin counting down from one hundred, until the numbers and equations stop swirling around in my head. I need this project to stay on course.

I pick up the phone and hit Eric's number. I get his voicemail, which doesn't shock me. He's been up to no good himself, no doubt putting his dick in someone even younger than the secretary Levi's after. I leave him a message telling him I need to push back our meeting. I have someone's granddaughter to threaten.

TWO

TREVOR

I PULL INTO THE SOUTH BLOCK OF FLANDERS BAY. My bay. Because I own it all. Except for one ratty old lot. When Eric and I first came up with the concept of Four Fathers, I knew exactly what I was going to do with my cut. For Eric, the money wasn't even a perk. He was raised with a silver spoon shoved so far up his ass, he probably just wanted the money to say he had it. I'm sure he was spending his earnings lining his toilet paper with gold so he could brag about wiping his ass with money.

When I made my first million, I bought a gigantic house—a place I never had growing up. After a while, it didn't feel right, so I bought another one. Then another one. Nothing I spent my money on offered me that feeling of home. I was trying to compensate for all the years I lived as a young child on the streets of Florida City, a low-income area near Miami, spending my nights around a bonfire off the beach. When I finally found myself in a place where I had a roof over my head, I expected to feel relief, but all I felt was trapped.

I park my car in the three-car driveway of the luxurious three-story beachfront home I just spent the last month renovating. The house itself is beautiful, but the previous owners were shit for decorators. Walking up to the door, I use my key to enter and look around at the work Darlene's done. Even though I want to strangle her half the time, she has a good eye for design. I drop the keys on the foyer bar and head to the back kitchen. Each and every house on this block opens up to the beach. At no time while you're in any part of these houses are you unable to get a glimpse of the water—exactly how I designed them. If the house didn't provide that, I had them reconstructed. Cost wasn't an issue—the perks of running a multi-billion-dollar freight company.

I pass through the white marble kitchen, appreciating

the new stainless-steel appliances Darlene put in. I requested the island be big enough to fit a solid twenty people around it, which she managed to make happen, and it looks fantastic.

To my right sits the exquisite twenty-person-table set ready to dine a royal army. Through the side windows, I notice the shutters to the eye sore next door have been pried open. The girl already seems to be settling in. I need to put a stop to this before she gets any more comfortable. I shoot a text over to Clara telling her I'm going to handle the girl instead.

I walk outside to the gigantic deck overseeing the sand and ocean. The ocean breeze across my face calms me, momentarily stopping the numbers running through my head. It's why I bought the houses where I did. To feel free at all, I need the ocean. I need the calmness of the waves. The smell of the salt water. The feel of the sand during the day when it's so hot it burns, or the coolness between my toes at night. I could have anything. Any house I want. And I want the openness of the ocean.

Obnoxious music blasts from the balcony next door, cutting through the quietness of the waves. "Jesus, what the hell is she listening to?" Kids these days and their terrible taste in music. I try to keep up with Kaden's changing tastes, but lord help me with the shit they come out with nowadays.

I pull at the collar of my dress shirt feeling the tightness around my neck. There's not a chance I'm waiting 'til the end of the summer to close on this deal. I don't care that the closing date states the first of August. This girl needs to sign this contract today. I can have a crew here within seventy-two hours. Every day she stalls, it's a setback. I look at the date on my watch. It's the first of June. Sixty-one days lost if she doesn't sign. Forty-three excluding weekends. Four hundred and eighty minutes, twenty-thousand and six hundred and forty—

I pull harder, breaking the top button off my shirt.

"Fuck."

She's fucking signing, whether she likes it or not. I'll hold her down for all I care. Too much time will be wasted. Seconds of wasted time. *Tick. Tick. Tick.* One million, five hundred and forty-eight hundred thousand minutes.

I turn around and storm back through the house and out the front door. Twenty-two feet across the front lawn and I make it onto her ratty front porch. The counting starts every time my closed fist meets her worn door. *One, two, three, four...* At seven banging seconds, she answers.

"Hi, can I help—"

"Sign the contract," I blurt out, trying to focus on the girl in front of me, who doesn't seem to be a girl at all. *Fuck.* Her ash blond hair blows across her oval shaped face with the evening breeze. Her eyes, the color of emeralds gaze politely back at me, as her full lips curve into a soft smile. My heart beats out of my chest. I should have popped a Xanax on my way over.

"Excuse me?" she asks, her voice light and sexy as fuck.

Focus, man.

"I said sign. The seven hundred-fifty thousand will be wired to your bank within an hour after we close. I can make that happen as early as tomorrow morning. Now, stop wasting my time." *Ten, nine, eight, seven...* God she has perky breasts. Her tight tank top hides nothing of her full C-cup. Perfect nipples. She's just under five-six, approximately six inches shorter than me. *Six, five...*

"I'm not signing anything. Like I told your realtor, I'm staying until the end of summer just like the original contract states. Now, if you'll excuse me—"

My hand goes out, stopping her from slamming the door in my face. *Four, three, two...* I should have taken the call from Dr. Winters this morning. The counting is getting worse.

"Excuse me! Remove your hand, sir, or I'll call the police!"

I snap out of my episode. *Sir?* Did she just call me sir? "What did you just call me?"

"I called you sir, and you're currently trespassing. Get off my property."

Jesus Christ, how old does she think I am? I look down at my chest peeking through where my button used to hold my shirt in place. Muscle. I see fucking muscle. I might be nearing forty-five, but I feel great. I *look* great. Not a single gray to be seen. I'm tan, smooth skin. My goddamn ex waxes my eyebrows for Christ's sake, and my dick works better than it did when I was a teenager. How the hell do I look like a *sir*?

"Hello? Are you deaf now?"

"Are you insinuating I'm old *and* can't hear?" She gives me a peculiar look while I look at her as if she's blind. Clearly, I'm not old. Or deaf.

"What? Maybe, but you're still on my porch."

"I'm not old enough to be called sir. Take it back." Apparently, I've resorted to child's play as well.

Her brows go up. "Seriously? You're offended I called you old?" Damn straight. I'm half tempted to show her just how not old I am by fucking her so hard over this ratty porch, the hinges break beneath us. "Hello? You sure you aren't deaf? You seem to also have a staring problem."

I can't deny that. I can't stop staring at her perfect lips tempting me to do so many things to them. *Jesus. When was the last time I got laid?* The numbers start at it again, counting down the months, hours, minutes from the last time I was with a woman. *Dammit.* "Stop," I burst out loud to my brain.

"No, *you* stop, you're the one staring."

"What? No, not you." This is turning out to be a big fucking disaster. I shove my hands over my face and through my thick dark hair while she observes my every move. A dumb part of me hopes she notices how thick my hair is. Someone who's old wouldn't have such a great head of hair.

Maybe I did this all wrong. Threatening her to sign the new contract may have not been the right angle. Maybe being a gentleman would have worked better. I try to start over.

"You're right. I'm sorry. Can I come in?"

Her eyes bug out at the question. Apparently,

that wasn't the right move either. "No. And no! You come banging on my door, threatening me, and—not gonna lie—creep me out with all your staring and number mumbling, then think you can come in? No, you most certainly *cannot*."

Dammit. I can't remember the last time I scared a chick. Because I never have. This girl must be blind. I start equating the amount of time I've been in her presence and how short the timespan of her ability to perform an adequate perception of me—

"You're doing it again!"

"Doing what?"

"Counting!"

What in God's name has come over me? I pull at my shirt again, needing more air down my chest. Speaking of chests, I seem to have a liking for hers, since I keep finding my eyes there. She catches on and crosses her arms over her tits, making them even perkier. *Fuck. Go home, Trev. Let Clara handle her.*

My dick wants me to do all the handling, but I'm

pretty sure the freaked out look on her face tells me I'm not impressing her enough to offer her to suck my cock as an apology.

I take a step back.

Then another one.

"Sign the contract. Take the money. Don't make me come back here." I threaten having to come back here, but my dirty mind fantasizes me doing just that. Sneaking into her bedroom, eating her raw, then fucking her bareback. I shake my head. What the fuck is wrong with me?

I turn, treading back across the lawn. *Seventeen, sixteen, fifteen...*

"Hey, Numbers?" her sexy little voice calls, and my head whips around. "You're wasting your time. I don't want your extra money. I'm not going to close any earlier than the original contract states."

"We'll see about that." I offer her my handsome, panty-dropping smile, then continue my path, counting the remainder of steps back to my house.

THREE

L U C Y

"**N**O, KATIE, YOU DON'T GET IT, HE WAS A WEIRDO. IF he hadn't opened his mouth, maybe it would be different."

"So, he was smokin' hot—old, but hot. And semi challenged? Is that what I'm getting? You move to Tampa for the summer to find yourself and meet a man and that's what you come up with?"

I laugh at her breakdown. "He's not challenged. He was just...interesting, I guess. He kept mumbling numbers. Like calculating everything he was saying. It was strange. But then again, he had this authority to him. This aura that screamed power. Control. It didn't make sense."

"Well, did you even ask how old he was? Age is just a

number nowadays, girl."

Ugh, she's kinda right. Jimmy, my ex, cheated on me, left me with a pile of debt, and tons of trust issues, and he was only a year older than me.

"Did he seem into you?"

"It doesn't matter. He's the one trying to push up the closing date on Gran's place. Not gonna happen. The last time we spoke, she made me promise I would come out here to find myself, so that's what I'm going to do," I say with more confidence than I feel. I hope I figure my shit out in two months. August first will be here before I know it, and I have a *lot* of shit to figure out.

Katie bursts out laughing through the phone. "What happens if the summer ends and you're still lost?"

"I'll go to the closing, sell the house they'll no doubt bulldoze, and come home." The ache already settles in my chest at the thought of letting Gran down. My parents died when I was in high school. My Gran raised me. I was heartbroken when she moved to their summer home in Florida, once shared with my Grandad before he passed, to spend out her retirement. Gran had begged me to come with her, but I was head over heels for Jimmy and the best I could do was manage an occasional phone call here and there. *Pathetic.*

When she fell ill, I told her I'd drop everything to take care of her. I owed it to her. But she lied and masked how sick she really was. But when I got the call, I knew. I got to spend a few days with Gran before she left me too. In that time, she lectured me about all the wrong decisions I'd made in my life. She had valid points. I was a walking hot mess. I was broke, heartbroken, and jobless, since I quit to spend the summer in Florida at their home—the home my grandparents owned way before Tampa became a hotspot for vacationers. I knew the closing didn't take place until the end of the summer, so I promised Gran before she died I would take some time for myself. And here I was.

"Damn. I hope that doesn't happen, since you picked up your entire life here in Minnesota to spend it on the beach. Do you even own a bathing suit?"

I laugh. I didn't as of two weeks ago when I officially made the decision to come to Tampa. Water has never been my thing, hence the hesitation when I learned Gran's house overlooked the ocean. "I doubt I'll spend too much time in the water. More like on the back deck reading my romance novels and sipping on some spritzers. Hey, maybe I'll even look for a part time job."

Katie gags before I even finish my sentence. "You did *not* go there to work. Relax. Read your smut. Get laid by a random—possibly your sexy, weird neighbor. But I'm pretty sure your gran didn't mean find work when finding yourself." True. But with my horrible track record, even searching for a man to get laid sounds like work.

I end up letting my friend go. The weather today is clear; not a cloud in the sky. I have high hopes of knocking out a whole book while catching some sun on the back deck. I've spent most of the week going through Gran's boxes of old photo albums, piecing together her life. There's no denying I shed a few tears at how happy my grandparents were and seeing old pics of my parents when they were young. I wish Gran were here to tell me stories behind some of the photos.

Being Sunday, I decide to take a break from memory lane. I snatch a worn historical romance paperback from Gran's bookshelf and slide into my brand new white bikini. Grabbing my towel and a Mike's Hard Lemonade from the fridge, I head out back.

The sun feels amazing on my skin. I inhale the breeze, tasting the salt of the ocean on my tongue. I drop my towel on the lawn chair and get comfortable. My shades are down, and my book is ready to be dominated.

"This is nice," I hum to myself, lifting my lemonade and taking a nice sip.

And out it all repels as I spit and choke on it.

"*Jeeeesus* Christ."

I knock my sunglasses halfway down my nose as my eyes threaten to fall out of their sockets. Where in holy heavens did *he* come from? The half-naked man leaning on his balcony across the way. My tongue about falls out of my mouth. *Is that Numbers? And holy shit, when did he get so much muscle?* I'd call him fit, but that's not fit. That's like, "Hi, I eat muscle for breakfast, lunch, and dinner, and now I'm just all muscle."

I wipe at my chin, unsure whether it's lemonade splatter or I'm drooling. I'm probably drooling. I wasn't paying attention to much of him yesterday when he was acting all crazy on my front step. I just wanted him gone. To be honest, while he was babbling, I was trying to dig in the back of my brain for my old high school karate moves in case he tried something on me. Looking at him now, I wish he had.

He lifts his hand, threading his large hand through his hair and dragging his fingers down his hard chest covered in a dusting of hair. "Oh boy, where's that hand going?" I mumble, licking my lips. Oh yeah. I see where this is going. Yep, oh yeah... *Did I just moan?*

Oh, hell yeah I did, but it's so worth it. His hand dips down into his board shorts and he adjusts himself. *Feel free to pull them down. Show us the goods,* I think, mentally visualizing just how big his junk is. He's a pretty big guy.

Big hands. Theory says, and all.

Watching him fondle himself in all his hot glory, my curiosity piques. How old is he really? He sure had a reason to take offense by my calling him old. He certainly doesn't *look* old. He surely looks a zillion times hotter than Jimmy, and he was only twenty-eight. I'm not an age wizard, but if I had to guess, I'd say late thirties, early forties. Definitely a bit out of my age range. Why? No idea. No real reason screaming stay away. Well, besides the major one being he wants to evict me, tear down my Gran's life of memories, and probably build a gym in its place.

Yeah, that's a good enough reason.

It also reminds me it's the guys who look appealing on the outside that usually turn out to be dicks on the inside.

His hand is still in his pants, and I can't imagine he's so large, it's taking him that long to adjust. Is he...he... *masturbating*! I lean forward, hoping a few more inches will give me a better prognosis. There's a peg in the way, so I twist to the side for a better view. His hand is still working. Oh, it stopped. It's pulling out. My eyes follow, until his hand is up his chest, rubbing at his—

"Oh *shit*!"

His eyes meet mine, and I jolt, dropping my lemonade, startling myself again when the bottle smacks against the deck and shatters. *Shit.* Did he just witness me gawking at him? I'm trapped, unable to pull away. He's sucking me in. *Pull away! Abort!*

The thing is, I can't. Dammit is he hot. He also looks mad. Probably so, since I kind of pulled a peeping tom on a personal moment.

"See something you like?" he calls over, confirming I'm busted.

"You two should get a room," I yell back, since there's no point in denying the fact that I *had been* watching, and I *had been* enjoying. I lean back in my chair, acting unfazed, even though my heartrate has picked up and a little tornado in my lower belly has my core on edge.

He breaks into a smile, but it's not an easygoing,

friendly smile. It's...predatory.

Jeeeesus.

Go back inside, Lucy. Stay clear.

"We're looking for a third if you want to come over and assist," he yells, causing the heat to spike. *Man, Florida weather is ridiculous.* I fan myself, blaming the ball of fire in the sky while picturing *myself* helping him out. I'm sure he's not thinking I'm as sexy right now with the look on my face. It's a face that's trying to determine if my small hand would even fit around his large package.

"What do you say? He's looking for a new friend."

I'm about to suggest a playdate, because he's got me super horny and clearly fogged in the brain, when two women in bikinis walk out.

What the fuck?

They take a place on either side of him, then snuggle closer, wrapping their arms around his waist. The one on my side leans in, laughing and whispering something in his ear.

You have *got* to be kidding me! What a prick! He pulls his eyes away from mine to reply to whatever the tramp said. What am I *doing*? Was I seriously just about to get played? Wow. Good to know my neighbor is a huge douchebag. I sit up quickly, grab my book, and stand. Avoiding the broken glass, I lift my eyes to the neighbor who's staring back, flip him off, then storm inside, forfeiting the sun, and sadly, the playdate.

FOUR

_____

T R E V O R

"I DON'T CARE, DARLENE."

"I know, but if you just let us use this property for the party, I promise I'll stay out of your hair." She squeezes my waist again, and I push her and Kiki off me. Jesus, these fucking women won't leave me alone. And they interrupted a possible introduction between my cock and sexy neighbor.

"You can't use the house. Last time I let you, it got trashed and one of your hooker friends started a fire in the kitchen."

Her pout drives me fucking mad. That shit used to work on me, when I disappeared for days at work and she claimed she needed a weeklong spa retreat in the Alps to forgive me. Who the fuck knows what she actually did on those trips. Knowing what I know now, I wonder if she's been muff diving longer than she admitted.

"I promise we'll behave."

"I said no. Now, you asked to use the house to lay on the beach. Do it before I kick you out. I have shit to do." And by shit, I mean figure out why that little firecracker just flipped me off, then figure out a way to get her to sign the contract and move the closing date up.

I push both women off me and walk back inside.

Heading to my room, the call I placed to my overpaid realtor pushes itself to the forefront of my mind. Clara had no luck. I pay her a shit ton not to come back and tell me she couldn't get the signature. I thought about going back over there and taking her hand and forcing her, but I was too much of a mess to handle it. I knew I should've called Dr. Winters and scheduled an appointment, but I wanted to be done with her. I was getting better. I didn't need her.

This week proved otherwise.

I knew I was starting to relapse when I went to work calculating the probability of seeing her when I left. The ratio of favorable outcomes had me at seventeen. The problem was, I didn't see her once. I was off, or she was hiding. But why? What was she doing in that shack? The list of those probabilities was so long. Over a hundred possible outcomes. By the time I laid my head down, forcing sleep, I was too far gone to do that. So, I went to the beach—a place I always seem to find solace. I swam, and jogged up and down the shore, hoping to exhaust myself. But the numbers kept forming.

I have no idea why I'm obsessing over this girl. She was in my presence for less than ten minutes and I can't get her out of my mind. I want that signature. But I want something else with it. I'm a man. Admitting I wanted my dick in her mouth isn't wrong. It's honest. I beat off to the thought of her sucking my cock more times than I could count. Literally. But my mind always went back to numbers. The probability of that outcome. Getting her to suck my dick. Fractions among fractions, thinking of all the ways to get that to happen.

I need to shut it down. She isn't as young as I imagined,

but she's still young. I'm guessing mid-twenties. Half my age. Not that age ever stopped me before. Pussy is pussy. But would she just be pussy to me?

She should be. I'm not in the right state of mind to get involved with anyone. I need to stay focused on the business. But having her watch me fondle my cock still has me at half-mast. I should go over there and force her to finish him off just for teasing me.

I shake my head. *Get a grip, asshole. Call Dr. Winters.* No. I can handle this on my own. I've been stressed before and dealt with it. I've been dealing with it my entire life. It wasn't until Jerald Winslow, a counselor from the shelter I had been visiting, took interest in me that I realized what I was. Or at least confirmed I wasn't retarded like my mother told me just before she left me on the beach, wanting nothing to do with me.

The center footed the bill for the testing. When the results came back stating I was a genius, everyone including me was shocked. A child prodigy they said. My level of output was that of an expert. I didn't know how or why I was able to do the things I did, but when numbers were involved, my brain just solved them. My memory was sharp. Algorithms, calculating speed, fractions built into fractions. It all came naturally to me. They said I was rare. I thought I was a freak. I didn't want this talent. I wanted to scrape the remnants of my visual vortex so the numbers would stop.

In the passing years of my young life, Jerald guided me. He helped me manage the stress of my mind. Taught me how to keep it at bay. And when it was time, he enrolled me in Harvard. I took the tests, stood in front of the university board, and got a scholarship.

Jerald Winslow saved my life. And I was forever indebted to him. He took me off the streets and made me feel more like a human than a freak. He gave me a home, even though I preferred the openness of the beach. The sand. He guided me where my own mother banished me. He saw me as a gift where my own mother saw me as a mutant.

Before I even bought myself a new pair of shoes, I

paid Jerald back for all the money he spent on me. For all the testing. I donated enough money to the shelter, the entire town could live there without fear of starving. I never had a father figure, but he was that to me. When he died, I relapsed. We were in our second year with Four Fathers and life was great. I was married and just had a son. When the shelter notified me there was an altercation with a homeless man and Jerald was shot, I about lost it.

I wanted revenge. I didn't care if I got killed or went to jail. I would have been in both those predicaments if Jerald hadn't saved me. It was my turn to find justice for him. But Eric set me straight. He got me into a clinic under watch until I was able to clear my head. That's when I met Dr. Winters. She taught me how to control my panic attacks. How to manipulate my mind when the numbers started to take control. And it helped. For the most part. Until recently.

I shove the memories to the back of my mind, walk into the master bathroom, and turn on the shower. Before

I try to sway my little neighbor, I need a cold shower and
a rough jack-off.

━━━

I'm coming up from the shore after a seven-mile run.
My muscles are on fire. My skin feels tight from all the
sand spitting up while I trekked along the coast. Walking
up to the outdoor shower under the deck, I kick off my
running shoes and step out of my running shorts. I turn
the nozzle and don't bother waiting for the water to
heat up. The coolness of the spray feels refreshing on my
sweaty skin.

I grab for the bar of soap and begin lathering up my
chest when I hear her. Well...hear mumbling. I turn to see
her walking down the worn steps of her deck and get a
burst of annoyance over the fact that she's even using the
back stairway. The house is old as fuck and those steps
are unsafe. With twelve steps, there's a probability of her
being able to use them ninety-two more times before
one breaking. The number of steps that can give out at

the same time are—

"You shouldn't use those stairs," I yell, startling her. She wobbles, grabbing for the banister, giving me another scare. The thing looks ready to fall off.

"Jesus, Numbers, you scared the piss outta me," she yelps, glaring at me like she wants to rip my head off. And I don't care, so long as she gets down those bunk stairs. That's when she starts bouncing on each step.

"Don't fucking do that. Those aren't safe," I snap back.

"Don't do what, this?" She jumps again, slamming her feet back down on another step. My anger spikes. Is she out of her fucking mind? Can't she see the stairs wobbling under her? She repeats the same gesture to the next two steps, giving me palpitations. The reoccurring effect has her falling through in less than seven more jumps. I glance over, noticing she's only using one hand to hold onto the railing and has a bottle in her other.

"Are you drunk?" I ask, now worried about her state of mind. She won't be able to catch herself if she falls.

"Super drunk actually. Thanks for asking. Now, mind your own business." She makes it to the bottom of the stairs. Relief washes over me as I watch her walk onto the sand and dig her toes into the cool pebbles of the sea. Then, she stumbles and trips. "Whoa! I'm okay!" she squeals, catching herself before she falls face-first into the sand.

I'm curious what she's up to. Until my mind figures it out. "You can't go in the water. It's not safe at night." I'm frozen, waiting for her to listen to me and turn back around. But she doesn't.

"Yeah, yeah, I've seen you in it all week at night. Nice try." She keeps walking. The tide has picked up the last couple days due to it being hurricane season. If I weren't trained to handle the choppiness of the waves, I wouldn't have been out there either.

"Yeah, and I know the water. You don't. Stay out of there," I demand. Why the fuck is she still walking? Christ, she's wobbling down to the water. The farther she gets, the harder it is to see her. The half-crescent moon glows against the water, but it's still so dark, I struggle to see anything but her silhouette. "Hey!" I yell, but this time, she doesn't respond.

I drop the bar of soap and run through the sand on high alert, listening for any signs of struggle. *What the hell is wrong with this girl?* Unsynchronized splashing. I go to call her name, but realize I don't even know it. Numbers, letters, and equations blast through my head at the chances I guess it right. It's undefinable, due to the various coed names—

"Hey!" I yell toward where I last spotted her. My feet slam into the sand, hitting the lining of the ocean shore and—

"BOO!"

I jump, losing my balance, and fall back into the cool ocean water.

"Holy shit! You should see your face!" She laughs. I wipe the water off my face as she stands above me, laughing, holding her chest. "Oh, man. For such a big guy, you sure do scare easily. I wish I recorded—"

Pushing to my feet, I tackle her, taking the last words right out of her mouth. She squeals as I bear hug her body to my chest and walk furiously with her in my tight hold into the cold water.

"Oh my God! Stop! It's freezing!" She kicks back and forth, trying to fight her way out of my grip. "Ahhh! Stop, please stop! It's fucking cold!" I don't stop until we're almost shoulder deep under. "Hold your breath." Her eyes shine in the moonlight, a battle warring behind them. She realizes my next move and doesn't know whether to yell or obey. My face remains stoic, serious, and she takes a deep breath as I sink us both beneath the water's surface.

When I pop back up, she has her arms and legs wrapped around me, the struggle forgotten. Her hair is soaked, covering her face. I lift my hand to brush it off, giving me the pleasure of her eyes. Green. Wide. She knows I'm lost in the sight of her. She seems to be doing the same. Her firm tits press nicely against my chest, and she has to be dumb not to feel my hard cock, even in the cold temperature.

It's then I remember I don't have any shorts on. A few seconds pass before she comes to the same realization. "Are you naked?" she asks, her voice hoarse. I can't help the urge I allow to happen. Using my hand gripping her taut ass, I press her into me. *Fuck, that felt good.* "Yep, naked," she whispers, her lids half closed. Her actions tease me, and I press into her again, gaining another reward. This time, her eyes shut and mouth parts. Hell knows what's changed between earlier today and now, but my dick tells me I should keep going until she tells me to fuck off.

"You okay with this?" I bend, putting my lips on her bare shoulder, and suck on her skin, which is softer than I expected.

"I don't like you, but I'm really horny and you're hot, so yep, let's do this."

Fuck. The mouth on her. Visual after visual of what I have in mind takes over. I bring my mouth to hers and kiss her with the ferocity of an untamed beast. Her mouth is sweet. Like cranberries and vanilla. She kisses me back, weaving her hands into my hair and tugging hard, causing a ripple effect in my dick. I want to fuck her right here in the water. Then I want to fuck her on the sand. Then my bed. Shit, I want to fuck her on my goddamn driveway. All the places my dick wants to be inside her swirl through my head.

But first, I want to taste her pussy. I don't remove my mouth from hers while I carry her out of the water and up the beach to my house. She's wild in my arms, her lips against mine, her cunt pressing into me...my dick is about to explode. I can't wait long enough to get her inside the house so I detour to the lawn chairs. Her back hits the cushion and a tiny squeal expels from her lips. I feel like a mad man unable to get to all of her fast enough. Ripping my mouth away from hers, I suck roughly down her chest to her breasts, pull back the tiny suit barely covering her tits, and bring her perky nipple into my mouth.

Fuck, I want to bite down. I want to bruise her. I want to own her.

I suck hard enough to receive another moan as her hands fly back into my hair. Her eagerness has me on fire. I let her go with a pop and work out the other tit. Once I'm satisfied, I bring my tongue down her stomach, past her navel, to the top of her pubic bone. My fingers fight not to tremble as I pull the string of her bikini bottoms. When they fall to the side, revealing her shaved pussy, I lose it. My mouth covers her, my tongue lapping her hard and fast. Just as expected, she tastes sweet as fuck. Her moans turn me on in a way that borderline scares me.

The things I want to do to her. Take her in every way possible. Her cunt, her ass, her mouth. I'm like a savage, eating her raw, using one finger to thrust inside her. Her hips lift off the chair, pressing her pussy into my face. Something snaps inside me, and I push two fingers in, thrusting harder while my tongue licks her clean. She's wet and soaking my face, and I can't get enough. Fuck, I can't stop. I want to fist her until she breaks. I push in a third finger and bite down on her clit. My cock is hard as stone. Once I actually fuck her, I know I'm not going to last long. Her moans become louder, heated, as her walls begin choking my fingers. She's going to come soon.

"That's it, baby. Fuck." I push harder and faster, unable to keep up with her as she fucks my fingers. I'm tempted to flip her and shove one up her ass. I bet that would be new for her. To watch her squirm... Dammit. I'm losing control. I push one last time, and she explodes. Her grip around my hand contracts as her orgasm blasts through her.

I pull out and crawl up her body, needing my dick inside her immediately. Her hooded eyes are fogged over. I push her legs wider, grab my cock, and place it at her slick pussy, reminding myself to go slow. I use her juices to wet my tip and thrust forward, all constraint gone.

"Fuck," I groan as her pussy sucks me in. She's so damn tight. Like perfection. I want to give her a moment to adjust to me, but I can't. "I've gotta move."

"Thank God. Fuck me." Her words set me ablaze. I start pounding into her, my balls slapping her ass. She feels amazing. With each thrust, her moans get louder.

Her hands move down, gripping my ass, and I growl deep in my throat. "Harder. Fucking harder," she begs, then brings her mouth to my shoulder and bites me.

And I fucking explode.

The animal living deep inside me erupts, and I lose it. I fuck her with all my strength, shoving her body into the cushion as I pound my dick in and out of her. Her teeth clench harder on my flesh, possibly breaking the skin, and my balls tighten. I don't want this to end, but this girl has me in a tailspin. I fuck her with haste until I know I'm done for. With one last shove of my dick, I groan and let go, exploding inside her.

"Jesus..." I breathe, rolling off her. My plan was to catch some of the cushion beside her, but she shoves me off, and I fall, smacking my back onto the deck. She's up and adjusting her bathing suit before I can even lift my bruised head off the ground.

"Where you going?" I ask, confused as she starts walking back to her house.

"Home. Thanks for the fun night, Numbers. See ya

around."

What the fuck?

FIVE ——

L U C Y

SITTING ON THE BACK DECK, I FINISH UP MY GROCERY list for all the things I'll need for my barbeque tonight. After running into Carol, the local seafood seller, yesterday, I spent all day scraping the old gunk off the grill and getting it back in working condition. She told me about her fresh seafood shack up the shore, and it got me craving some grilled lobster. My budget told me to stick to peanut butter and jelly sandwiches and ramen noodles, but maybe splurging once wouldn't hurt. I promised myself I'd stick to ramen the rest of the month to make up for the hit I'd take buying lobster tails. Plus, she convinced me she'd give me a great deal being a new customer. Game on.

With the list now complete, I take a rewarding sip of

my coffee, appreciating the view. Gran must have loved it here. Waking up to the beautiful ocean waves. The warm sun against her face while she lost herself in thought. I've only been here a short time, but it's starting to set in why she made me promise to come out here.

And she was right to do so. The last few years, I've struggled with finding clarity—figuring out what I wanted out of life. I was in and out of jobs and boyfriends. I couldn't pinpoint my purpose. I had dreams, aspirations, but I also had a short span for responsibility. I spent too much time trying to please everyone around me, I forgot to find pleasure in myself. I let guys walk all over me. Coworkers. Life. I just needed a change.

Gran knew it too. When I got here, there was a letter on the kitchen counter addressed to me. I recognized her handwriting right off the bat. But I've yet to open it. I know it's going to be a gut-wrencher since it's the last letter she wrote me, but decided I would open it when I felt the time was right. I've been here over a week, and yeah, haven't touched it. One of these days, I'm going to man up and read her last words. But right now, I'm going to focus on today. Specifically, tonight's dinner. *Speaking* of dinner, I get a move on it.

Taking a large sip of my coffee, I turn my head as my eyes peek over the rim of my mug at the neighbor's house. Geez, what was I thinking? My vagina tells me, "Who cares? That was the best sex of my life." My brain says it wasn't smart. I mean, I let a stranger blow his load inside me for crying out loud. But I'm on the pill, and obviously living on the edge, so whatever. All I know is I swear I saw Jesus as I came, and I've been walking with a limp since Sunday. It's Tuesday, and I still can't walk straight. I had way too many lemonades and decided to take Katie's advice and live a little. Have random sex—*check*. I didn't go down to the water expecting all that to happen, but thank God it did.

A part of me feels like walking over there and thanking him for setting me straight—or lopsided, as the case may be, since I'm pretty sure he dislocated my hip with his dick. I'm also seriously considering asking him to do it again. You know, to fuck my hip back in place. And then I realize I'm insane.

He's the bad guy, Lucy! And he is. I had to take a hose to some guy yesterday who was trying to take measurements of the property lines. Inspections aren't scheduled until late July. It's just one more thing he's trying to do to push things along. He might be a bomb-ass lay, but he's still the enemy. And I don't care how fantastic his monster dick is, it's not going to get me to move the closing date any sooner.

Besides that, it's clear he's a playboy. Monday morning, when I stepped outside to get the paper, I noticed a woman walking up his driveway. I threw myself inside my own door before he opened his so he wouldn't see me. Was I mad he had another woman over so soon after giving me not one, but two explosive orgasms? I mean...no. *Yes.* I wasn't! I'm a big girl. We're both adults here. I needed to release an entire department store of hormones, and he needed to pound me into his lawn chair. Which now has me leaning over to check to see if it's broken. No one would be shocked if it were at least bent. 'Cause, I mean...

I shake my head. For real. Don't care. This summer is about me and taking for once. And that's what I did. I took his huge cock and used it hardcore. I look down in my coffee mug, wondering if I accidently poured booze in here. My thoughts aren't normally so brash.

I stand, dumping the remainder over the railing, when I get my first glimpse of him since the other night. He's dressed in a grey suit, his crisp dress shirt missing a tie. Just like the last few times I've seen him, minus Sunday night. He's in flip flops, though, not dress shoes.

"Such a strange dude," I say to myself. He starts to turn toward me, and I thank God I'm a ninja. I jump through my sliding glass door and lift my head up through the window of the kitchen, only to duck when I find him looking over here. *Did he see me?* No way. Ninja skills. He stares a bit longer, until something else gets his attention. A woman walks out onto the deck, hands him something, then leans in and kisses him on the cheek.

Ugh. Playboy.

━━━━

One thing Tampa clearly doesn't lack is good looking men. Just walking down the beach, I claimed about four hot guys and did them all in my head. By the time I make it to the seafood shop, I feel like I need a cigarette and a nap.

"Ah, I see you listened!" I turn to the cute little lady I met the other day.

"I sure have. Gonna make this dinner my bitch tonight."

"Excuse me?"

Grow up, Lucy. "Oh...uh, nothing. Gonna make some delicious dinner tonight. So! Whatcha got?"

She sticks out her hand, pointing to the entrance, and we head into her shop. The place is tiny, but jam packed with refrigerated display cases surrounding the outside and aisles of dry foods filling the middle space. I fight not to cover my nose at the overwhelming smell of raw fish. Maybe I should have stuck to burgers—

"You get used to it after a while."

I turn to my left, not realizing anyone else was in the shop. A guy—I think number three on my mental do-me list—stands super close to me.

"Oh yeah, sorry. Not used to the fish smell. Where I come from, it's normally already dead and wrapped in a pretty seal and probably pumped with tons of chemicals... Okay! So, hi. I think I just saw you on the beach. Are you a local?" I hope I just saved myself from looking like a complete idiot.

His smile is kind of to die for. Like most of the guys I've seen, he's wearing a set of board shorts and a T-shirt that's a wee bit too tight. Not that I'm complaining.

"You can say that. I live not too far away. And you?"

"Oh, I'm not from here. Well, I am now. Or for the next two months." *Seriously?* This guy has my tongue all twisted. "I'm staying here for the summer." *There. Gah!*

He smiles wider, taking another step closer. For a

quick second, I think he's about to reach for me, when he leans past, grabbing a box of rice off the shelf in front of me. "Well, welcome to the neighborhood..." He pauses.

Oh! "Lucy. The name's Lucy." I stick my hand out, and he takes it, shocking me when he brings it to his lips and presses a kiss to the top.

"Pleasure meeting you, Lucy."

"All right, my darling!" The little lady steps between us, handing me a box. "You'll make a great meal with these two. Make sure to come back again soon for more seafood."

I smile at the woman, bringing my eyes back to my new hot friend. "Lobster night."

"I see."

Okay, so... "Well, it was nice meeting you, uh..."

"Jax."

"Got it. Jax. Well, hope to see you around!"

"Oh, I hope so too." And then, he's gone. He drops the box of rice on the counter as he walks out and down the beach where he came from.

Tampa dudes are strange.

———

"This is not what I had in mind." I stare down at the two live lobsters in the box on my deck. I expected lobster tails, as in, already dead and cut off for me to just sprinkle some salt and pepper and throw on the grill. Did *not* plan for alive.

"What do I even do with you two?" I've never killed anything before. I'm not planning on today being the day I start either. Disappointment smacks me hard. I just spent money on a dinner I'm going to end up putting in my bathtub, naming, and caring for until they outlive their lives. "You look like a Herald." I point to one. "We'll call you Bill."

"Who's Bill?"

I whip my head up to see Numbers walking up my stairs. He seems to have ditched the suit for a pair of shorts and a white V-neck. If I had a choice, I'd pass on the lobster and have him for dinner.

"Bill, my new pet lobster." He makes it to the top, his large frame dominating my small deck. He leans down to inspect my box.

"You're naming your dinner?"

"Well, it's not my dinner anymore. They're my pets now. I don't believe in animal cruelty. So, meet Herald and Bill. They'll be staying with me for a while." Like, however long their life—

"Ninety-two years. Give or take a year."

"Huh?"

"Ninety-two years. How long they'll live. Imagining they're matured enough by age five to eight to sell for a decent market price. Their full lifespan is up to one hundred years. If you plan on keeping them as a pet, you'll have them for another ninety-two years. Give or take a year or two."

"Seriously?" I look down at my new friends and realize I'm not financially capable of keeping a pet, let alone two, for the next ninety plus years. I look back at Numbers. "Where do you come up with this stuff?" If I weren't secretly ogling him, I would've missed the quick flash of stress on his face.

"Simple facts. You live off the ocean, you know a little bit about lobsters."

"Hmmm," I hum in response. I can't seem to stop looking at him, hoping he'll keep talking so I have a reason to be staring at him. His shirt is way too small for him. Or maybe he's just too big for the shirt. Either way, his muscles are bulging. Must be a Tampa thing. His board shorts fit nicely, even though he could use an extension in the crotch region since it looks like the poor guy is suffocating. *Oh my God, lift your eyes!* I do so, catching his smirk. No doubt, I just got caught staring at his junk. He doesn't call me out, which I'm thankful for. Instead, he goes on again with his numbers. He's not loud about it, as if he doesn't realize he's counting. And it's not just numbers. It's like he's repeating math problems.

"Okay! Well, thanks for the lesson. I'm...just gonna go inside and make my bathtub into their new home." I bend down to grab the box.

"Here, let me help you." He leans in, giving me a whiff of his cologne. He smells amazing. I want to tell him I've totally got this, but my mouth locks when he reaches down and his arm flexes as he wraps his hand around the box. I watch in slow motion as each finger squeezes the sides, remembering those bad boys ramming into me.

"Wanna lead the way?"

"To what?" I blurt, forgetting what was happening. *Lobsters. Home.* Right. It's not helping that my hormones are once again skyrocketing. I've plowed through three erotic romances in the last twenty-four hours and there's nothing more I'd like to do than reenact some of those filthy scenes with the man in front of me. "Oh, yeah...uh, this way."

I lead him inside through my mess. I'm not much of a cleaner. Or an organizer. *Or one who enjoys laundry*, I think as I pick up a pair of dirty underwear and toss it out of sight. I feel the heat follow us through the tiny hallway leading to the even smaller bathroom, then stop at the door and lean against the wall for him to walk past me.

He's so big, it's no shock our bodies are forced to touch as he maneuvers into the tiny space. My nipples are super hard, and I take a quick look at his shirt, making sure I didn't rip a hole in it when he brushed against my tits.

"I'll...uh, just put them in the tub?" he asks, and I nod. *Put them in the tub and run. Or I'm gonna do something I'll probably regret.* I really need to lay off those books. He drops the box, then bends down to pick up Herald—or is it Bill?—before dropping each into their new home.

I have absolutely no idea what is really happening. I'm too busy staring at his ass. His tight ass cheeks I remember squeezing like a stress ball just before Jesus paid me a visit.

"You may want to carry some seawater up here, to keep them happy." He stands, moving out of the small bathroom. Stopping in front of me, he says, "They tend to live longer when—"

I'm on him like a cat attacking catnip.

I jump just high enough for him to quickly get the

hint and catch me, lifting my legs around his muscled waist. My lips reach up and attack his, kissing him just like Fabio kissed his princess in *The Dirty Lord*—my latest read.

The best part is, he's on me just as fast. His mouth opens and our tongues collide, suckling at one another like two teenagers in heat. I feel the thump as his back hits the wall. His hands coddle my ass. I'm not shocked he's already hard and grinding into me. He seems to keep that thing that way.

There's a small chance I'm going to regret this, but a *way* bigger chance I'm going to be patting myself on the back later.

He removes a hand from my ass and brings it up my back before wrapping it into my hair. When he's got a good hold, he squeezes and pulls my head back a smidge, allowing better access to my lips. His tongue takes over, swirling around and fucking my mouth. I moan, so turned on and overheating.

"Bedroom." It's all I need to say. He pushes off the

wall and takes long strides before falling back on the small mattress. With him on the bottom, I'm in control, and it delights me to know I get to take the wheel this time. My mind has been in the gutter ever since Sunday night, and I'm so sick of masturbating. Having him under me to do as I please excites me.

I raise my body, pressing my hands to his chest. He really is built like a brick house. I scoop my fingers under his shirt and tug. "Shirt's gotta go." He's up instantly, and the shirt is gone.

Jesus. I must have done something right to earn this one.

"Your turn," he says.

Only fair. I lift my tank over my head and toss it to the side. His hands are on my tits instantly, and I couldn't be happier. He kneads my nipples between his thumb and index finger while I tug at his shorts. "Off we go," I say, losing my power of authority. His simple teasing is getting me going faster than I'd like. I might even settle for some dry humping to get off.

He's a smart man and lifts his hips so I'm able to drag his shorts down, almost getting whipped in the face with his gigantic dick. God forbid we never make it to the good part because he blinds me in one eye beforehand.

"Your turn," he repeats. *Sure thing*, I think as I stand up on the bed and step out of my jean shorts. I pull my underwear down with them, bypassing the bashfulness of him seeing me naked. This is just sex. No time for overthinking.

I drop back down, crawl up, and kiss him. His lips are plump and inviting. I make good use of my hands, touching his pecs, abs, and working downtown to direct traffic, as in get the big guy inside. I'm rewarded when I reach his cock and wrap my small hand around him. He's smooth to the touch. Large. I kiss him harder, anticipating what's to come. I've been on edge the past two days; I don't have time for foreplay. I'm already wet— no shocker—so I settle him where he needs to be and slide down. I'm not sure who moans first. It sounded like a tie. I want to tell him I won, because I'm competitive like that, but he starts working his hips, thrusting into me.

"Your pussy is fucking perfect," he groans, gripping my hips and lifting me up and down on his cock. "You just suck me up." He lifts me again, and slams me back down.

"Gobble, gobble," I moan, feeling like his dick possibly just hit a rib. I also forfeit trying to rehash what just came out of my mouth. *Gobble, gobble? Really?*

"Fuck, I gotta flip you," he grunts, and *whoospie daisies*! Before I have a chance to argue, I'm on my back, and he's thrusting me into the mattress. My legs wrap around his waist, holding on for dear life as I moan, groan, and almost cry out in ecstasy. *Fuck, fuck, fuck!* Each time he slams into me, my eyes roll back. I fear I'm going to choke on my own tongue. We're both starting to sweat. I can feel his skin getting clammy when I grab for his ass and squeeze. "Jesus Christ," he growls, his balls slapping my ass for good behavior. There is one thing I like about him, and it's that he doesn't take things slow. Neither time has he tried to woo me—which is far from what I want or need. I need to be fucked. And he is doing a fantastic job of it.

Pounding into me again, he reaches between us and pinches my clit. I throw my head back and break. I moan in silence, since my throat is bone dry, and cry out my release, my back arching off the bed.

One, two, on the third hard thrust, he comes, pushing my back up the mattress.

His body falls on top of mine.

We're both breathing heavily. Him more than me, since I can't really breathe at all with his heavy frame on me. I give it a few more seconds before the awkwardness settles in, then tap him on the butt. "Okay, well...I have to go check on my new friends, so..."

Thankfully, he doesn't ask questions as he pulls out and stands. I feel his semen dripping out of me. Fuck. I need to be smarter than this. I get up without making eye contact, and grab for my tank top and shorts. "So, I'm just gonna go...I'll see ya around." I walk out of my bedroom to the bathroom, forgetting I was already in my place.

Idiot.

SIX

TREVOR

"YOU LISTENING TO ME?"

I pull myself back from my thoughts to Eric, who's sitting across from me in the conference room. "Yeah, got it. Warehouse turnover creates forty-two percent profit margin for the company. If we add fifteen new trucks, picking up the thirty-seven new routes, that brings in an annual income of fourteen billion."

Eric smiles. He's pleased with the figures, and if they're coming from my mouth, he knows they're solid. The new warehouse addition is going to be a success.

"You okay, man?" he asks as I start falling back into my thoughts.

"Fine," I grit out. "Why wouldn't I be?"

"Because I know you. I know the signs. You've been

distant. Counting out loud again. Do you need to see Dr. Winters?"

I instantly become agitated. I love Eric, but I don't need him acting like my father. "I'm fine. Just have some shit going on with the Flanders property." And boy is that a goddamn understatement. My problem is less with the unsigned contract and more with the spitfire girl staying in it.

I went over there yesterday to talk about what happened Sunday night. Instead, we had round two of mauling each other. She was nothing I was used to. She was also disrupting my very organized life. The counting was getting worse. But it always revolved around her. Watching her in the morning. Every time I would see her pass by her kitchen window. The seconds it would take to pass by again. It's like I'm obsessed with her. But that isn't me.

I won't admit to Eric that I already met with Dr. Winters. She came by the house Monday morning and guided me through the cloudiness in my head, which helped. But then I fell right back into it when I walked into that shack and got my brains fucked out by the little sex goddess. The strange thing was, whenever I was deep inside her, the numbers stopped. Nothing but quiet inside my head, allowing me to enjoy her. But then I would go home, where my brain would reset, fighting every single equation, probability, and factor of what had just occurred and the likeliness of it occurring again. I wanted her. But strangely, I wasn't sure she wanted me. My dick, yeah. But past that, she showed no interest. And that fucking bugged me. So, tonight, after work, I'm going to go over there to demand answers.

What's even more shocking is not once since Sunday have I thought about the setback of the delayed closing of the property.

I leave Eric to finish the paperwork, knowing he's in his own shit of woman problems—or should I say child problems, since that's how young he prefers them. I make it home seventy-two seconds faster than normal and pull into my driveway. I notice the open windows next door, so I shut off my Aston Martin, get out, and walk over.

I bang three times on the door with no response. I know she's in there, so she better not even think about trying to avoid me. When I bang again, and she doesn't answer, I twist the knob. It moves freely in my hand, and I push the door open, ready to call her name, when the fucked-up thing hits me. I don't even know it. I've been balls deep in her twice now, and we've never exchanged names. I make a mental note to change that.

I walk further into the old house, peeking down the small hallway. Nothing. I walk through the kitchen and find her outside on the deck.

"Hey, I knocked," I start, pushing through the sliding glass door to find her sitting with her legs crisscrossed on her old lawn chair in tears. "What's wrong? What happened?" I'm on high alert, ready to kill anyone who's messed with her.

"What are you doing here?" She sniffles, blowing her nose into a beat-up tissue.

"I wanted to talk. Why are you crying?"

She starts to cry harder, and I fumble for a moment, not knowing what to do. I'm shit when it comes to women and emotions, so I wing it and sit down on the open chunk of cushion, bringing my hand to pat her back. "Hey, whatever it is, it's gonna be okay."

"No, it's not," she sobs, throwing her head into my shirt and soaking it. I'm starting to get agitated that someone really upset her. Hurt her in some way. The array of what could have happened builds in my head. What I can do to retaliate. "He's dead," she cries into my shirt.

I pull her off me, worried. "Who's dead?"

"Herald. Or Bill. I'm not sure which one. The other one won't tell me." And she's back in my chest sobbing.

"The lobster?" I ask, now confused.

"Yeah. I came home, and he wasn't moving. I tried to get answers from the other one, but he wasn't talking. I killed him. I murdered a helpless animal." And off she goes again. She's bawling over killing a lobster? Jesus, this girl. I'm not sure whether to laugh or roll my eyes.

Seeing how upset she is, I hold back from doing both. I adjust her so I get a better fitting on the chair, and lift her, placing her in my lap. I wait until her cries are more of a whimper and I can feel her breathing calm.

"You okay?" She doesn't immediately pull away, which I'm fine with. Strangely, I like the feel of her in my lap.

"Yeah, sorry. I've just never killed anything before. I wanted to give them a better life." This girl. This time, I do smile. I move her hair away from her face. "I'm sorry. I kinda soaked your shirt."

I look at her, not giving a fuck about my shirt. "It's just a shirt."

"Yeah. Well, I should probably get off your lap. I'm wrinkling your nice pants."

"Fuck my pants," I tell her, and a haze starts to form in her eyes. My little minx is getting heated. Before this goes any further, I shut it down. "Let me take you to dinner. Where you don't have to worry about the preparation."

I may have shocked her. "You wanna take me to

dinner?"

"Dessert too, if you're good." Her smile pleases me. It's been a while since something so simple did that. It used to be pleasing Eric, making money, working figures, but that got old fast. It quickly became a task. Four Fathers is everything to me, but the luster in it died a long time ago. I should be thankful for the money—for not being on the streets anymore. I should indulge in the billions I'm sitting on like the other partners do. But it's not about money to me. Yeah, I blew my first billion on buying an entire subdivision just to have the quietness of the beach, but that's what I needed to survive—to find solace from the fucked-up shit swirling in my head.

"You're counting again."

Shit. When I get in my head, I forget I lose focus and do that. "Sorry. So, what do you say? Will you let me feed you?"

Her smile fucking does shit to me. "As long as it's not lobster."

Fuck, I'm in trouble with her.

———

"So, can I ask you a question?"

"Anything you want." I learned on the ride over to Flemings, one of Tampa's hottest steak houses, her name is Lucy. She strangely already knew mine, telling me she figured it out by searching the name on the contract, then proceeded to google me, needing to know what she was up against with my pushing the early sale of her Gran's house.

"What's with the counting? If you don't mind me being nosy."

I knew this was coming. "There's nothing wrong with me, if that's what you're thinking." I watch her eyes fill with guilt. They always pin me first with an illness. "I'm what you call a math prodigy. My mind works solely based on numbers. Anything that is probable and can be solved, my brain latches onto it and tries to solve it."

I watch her try to dissect the information. "It means my mind never stops. I'm always counting. Steps, seconds between breaths, the distance between waves. It can be anything, and my brain wants to break it down."

"How...how do you function with all that madness?" She catches her choice of words. "Shit, I'm sorry, I didn't mean—"

"No, it's fine. Some days are easier than others. Certain things trigger it. Stress is a number one reason. I learn to deal with most of it, but when it gets bad, I use methods that have been taught to me over the years to calm my mind."

"Wow. That's nuts. So, like, can you tell me how many words you just spoke?"

"Seventy vowels, fifty-seven syllables, sixteen verbs, and twelve nouns in the last minute and a half."

"Jesus, how did you remember all that?"

"It's just the way my mind works. I can't really control it. So, I just learn to live with it." She's quiet for a bit, so I take that opportunity to turn the spotlight on her. "Tell me about you. What brought you out here?" Her beautiful smile falls at my question. "You don't have to answer—"

"Nope. You answered mine. Only fair. My Gran died. It was her last wish to have me stay here over the summer to help sort my life out."

"And do you need sorting?"

"I need so much sorting, I doubt just the summer is going to fix me."

"What's wrong with you?" I ask, curious since I find her to be pretty perfect.

"I'm a mess. I have no direction. I make poor choices, and I can't for the life of me follow through with anything. She wants me to find my way, I guess. Find love. Find my true passion, whatever that is. Her dying wish was just for me to be happy. And she thought having me spend the summer here would do that."

My stomach turns with guilt. It reminds me of the addendum I grabbed off my desk and shoved in my suitcoat pocket when I left the office. I'm not even sure why. I had no intentions of approaching the subject with her. The last thing on my mind was giving her any reason to leave. And now, listening to her, I couldn't even imagine doing that. I push it farther into my pocket as the waitress comes by to take our order.

We enjoy a great meal over small chatter. I learn she's twenty-seven, and confess my own age. I thought she would be turned away by it, but it didn't seem to bother her. We keep the topics light, and before I know it, three hours have passed and we're getting the check.

"Are you sure I can't help pay?" she asks for the billionth time as we walk to my car.

I take her hand and open the door, helping her in. "I wouldn't think of it. It was my treat." I also know from the small chatter she is completely broke. I had to reign in my anger hearing that she's been living off sandwiches and cheap noodles since she got into town. Then again, maybe if she let me buy her damn house already, her money problems would be solved. Not to mention, all the restaurants in town I could have been spoiling her with.

The ride home is quiet. I take the scenic route

along the coast, and she rolls down all the windows, allowing the ocean breeze to blow through her hair. As soon as I pull up in my driveway, she turns to me, gifting me with the most beautiful smile. Her hair is a complete rat's nest, making her even more irresistible. I told myself I wasn't going to pull another dick move and treat her like the two times we've been together. It's different now.

I jump out and go around the other side to help her, but she's already climbing out. I take her hand so she doesn't stumble, since she's been drinking and close the door.

"Well...thanks again. I really enjoyed tonight. I needed it after...ya know."

I smile back at her, nodding. "Anytime."

We stand there in an awkward stare down, waiting on each other to make a move. If she doesn't, I won't. I want this to be something she wants.

"Okay. Well...goodnight then," she says, starting to turn.

"Goodnight," I reply, watching her ass sway in the

cute little summer dress she wore while regretting allowing her out of my grasp. I turn to head inside when I hear her call my name. Before I fully regard her, she's on me. My arms move on instinct, catching her. Her lips are on mine, and we kiss like two lovers who have been apart for years. I press her taut body harder against me as our tongues tangle, fighting at one another, and carry her into the house.

I continue to kiss her as I walk down the long marble hallway to the stairs leading to the second level. As we enter the master, I realize the room is equivalent to the size of the shack she's staying in. My mood plummets for a second knowing how unsafe that place must be. The probabilities of the structure—

"You're doing it again," she mumbles against my lips as I bring her up to the king size bed and drop her. The way she squeals and her blonde hair spreads along her face like a fucking angel...I want to freeze this moment— keep her here like this for as long as I can. Her deviant smile breaks the moment. It's time to fuck her.

"I'm hoping that serious look is because you're calculating how hard you're going to fuck my brains out."

My smile isn't sweet like hers. It's predatory. Dangerous. I want nothing more than to fuck her until she loses sight of anything but me and my aching cock. "I'm going to fucking devour you."

And then, I snap.

I grab her thighs, causing her to fall back, and pull her ass all the way down until her legs are hanging off the bed. My need to have my mouth wrapped around her wet cunt is unbearable. Pushing her dress up, I grab at her thong and rip it off. I plan on buying her a whole closet's worth. Wasting no time, I'm in her, devouring her, tasting her sweet juices on my tongue. I suck so hard, I fear hurting her, but her thrashing under my hold tells me my little minx is enjoying herself. Her body starts to tighten, and I know she's about to come on my mouth. The moment she explodes is pure ecstasy for me. That doesn't stop me from sucking until long after her tremors have settled. She melts in my grip, but I'm nowhere near done with her. I pull away, removing my clothes. She starts to climb up, but I stop her.

"Not so fast. I want you on the bed. Turn over. Kneel." My demands are immediately met. She flips her body and gets on all fours, sticking her ass out at me. *God help me I don't lose control and take this too far.* Undoing my belt, I drop my pants, and my cock flies out hard as stone.

I grab onto her hips, pulling her to my dick. Her little moans tell me she's anticipating what's in store. *Well, that makes two of us.* "Tell me what you want," I taunt, pressing the top of my cock into her wet opening. She moans again and grinds her ass into me. If she doesn't watch it, my dick is going to go in her ass instead.

"I want you to fuck me," she purrs. *Dammit, she fucking purrs.* My dick jolts, wanting deep inside her. Her ass is fucking with me, and I need to concentrate. "Do you want me to beg? I will, I'm horny and wet and I want your cock so far up me, I can feel you choking my throat—"

I slam so hard into her, she chokes on the last of her

words. She turns me on so bad, I can't take it. I pull out and slam just as hard—if not harder. Grabbing her ass cheeks, I dig my fingers hard into her skin and ride her, each moan giving me the fuel to take her rougher. Deeper.

"Oh, fuck yes, deeper."

Jesus, she's perfect. I raise my hand and slap her ass hard enough to leave an immediate welt. She groans, squeezing around me. A long, pleasurable moan follows, and I want to spank her ass until her entire cheek is red with my mark. In and out. Harder and rougher. My mind is clear. All I care about are the sounds falling from her mouth. I've lost track of how many times I've spanked her. How many times she's begged me to go deeper. I suck a finger into my mouth, then bring it to her back hole. Without a second thought, I shove the digit in her ass.

"Oh, my fucking God!" Her foul-mouthed curse mixed with a moan has me swelling to max capacity inside her. I've never been so turned on. So hard. So thick with the need to take everything from her and make her mine. She pushes hard against my finger, encouraging me. I pull out and shove it back in, that sweet moan filling the room.

"You like that, you naughty minx?" I pull my cock out and punch it back, along with my finger. In and out in unison, I become lost in the moment. I swear, the next time I take her, it's going to be in that sweet ass of hers.

Her pants shorten as she clenches around me, crushing my cock.

"Oh, oh. Oh!"

"FUCK." My orgasm takes me by surprise, blasting through me so fast, I almost lose my footing. My knees threaten to buckle as I try to pump into her one more time, spilling every last ounce of cum deep inside her.

SEVEN

L U C Y

I'M CONVINCED THIS BED IS MADE OF PURE HEAVEN. Clouds stuffed into a mattress made to offer me the best sleep ever. I snuggle even farther into the feathered comforter, swearing an army will have to rip me away if they ever want me to leave it.

I turn to my side and get the best visual. Trevor on his back, sleeping. His mouth slightly parted, the bedsheet resting just below his naval. And *meow*, does he look hot. I mentally high five myself for landing such a great guy. At first, it was just about sex. He's a knockout looks wise and in bed, but last night at dinner, getting to actually know him with his clothes on, was pretty awesome. He's smart and funny, and learning about his numbers issue was intriguing.

It was a mood killer for a quick second when he mentioned a snippet about his childhood. What kind of mother just abandons her own blood? It made me want to find her and kick her in her shitty crotch, but when he talked about the man who saved him, and then his partner Eric, I backed off on my secret plan. After that, the rest of the convo was light. Favorite music, food, dislikes—stupid shit to keep us from hitting any deeper topics, I'm sure. He seemed nervous when I tried to bring up anything heavier than my love for cereal and pop music. Then again, I was fine with it.

Man, I can stare at him all day. He's seriously gorgeous. His lips—God, he has magical lips. They're plump and soft. The things they can do. *Lordie*. I wonder how someone like him is still single.

I smile like a schoolgirl thinking about how amazing last night was, and where he explored. Definitely unchartered territory, but holy smokes, it had my orgasm hitting a whole new level. I'm not gonna lie, I did panic for two seconds thinking he was going to hit me with his large-and-in-charge dick, but after the little test drive, I'm curious to try the full course.

There's a sudden blush to my cheeks at the thought of how to wake him up. He looks so peaceful, like it's the first sleep he's gotten in years. My body feels like complete mush, but sitting on his face would be worthwhile.

"I hear you giggling, what are you up to?"

His eyes slowly open. God, put eyes on the list of magical features. "I was just thinking of ideas on how to wake you up, but you looked so peaceful, I was starting to feel guilty for all the ways I was going to ruin that for you." He turns to his side, no doubt offering me a fantastic view of his scrunched pecs. *Yum.*

"And what did you have in mind?" he asks, his voice still hoarse from sleep, and so, so sexy.

I smile like a little girl, embarrassed to put a voice to the ideas floating around in my head. They're pretty naughty. I open my mouth to start with a PG-rated idea when his phone goes off. That damn thing has been going off all morning.

"Someone misses you. That's like the fifth time it's gone off."

He turns, finding the clock on the nightstand. "Fuck." He sits up, grabbing his phone.

"Everything okay?"

"Yeah." He scrolls through the missed calls. "I seemed to have slept is all."

I laugh. "Is that a new thing?" I was under the impression all humans slept.

"Uh, yeah. I—I have trouble sleeping." He continues to scroll, then puts his phone to his ear to listen to a voicemail. "Shit."

"Are you in trouble? Did you need to go into work?"

He looks at me, gifting me that sly smile. "I'd be lying if I said Eric doesn't sound pissed. I missed the morning meeting for our new warehouse." He drops his phone and tackles me. My back hits the mattress as his body covers mine. "But he can wait. I have more important things to take care of." He brings his lips down on mine and offers me the best good morning kiss ever.

I throw my wrinkled summer dress back on, minus my underwear since they didn't make it last night. Trevor hits the bathroom, telling me he'll meet me in the kitchen. He claims to be a pretty good cook, so a breakfast of champions is in order. This I'm excited for since I'm starving.

I walk out into the foyer, enjoying how awesome the house is. It reminds me of this show I'm obsessed with on HGTV, Million Dollar Listing. I take out my phone and snap a few pictures to send to Katie. She would never believe the house I'm in. I take one of the chandelier, betting it's real crystal and costs more than I'll make in a lifetime, when the front door opens.

"Honey, that top looks great on you. Your boob job is healing nicely."

I watch in confusion as two women barge into Trevor's house. "Uh...hi, can I help you?" I ask, hoping they have the wrong house. Getting a better look, they do seem familiar. The two women Trevor had over the other morning.

"Oh, we're here for Trevor. Are you renting one of his houses? They're all great locations. The beach at night is lovely." They walk past me and through the kitchen to the back deck.

And *that's* why he's single. Because he's a playboy. *Idiot.*

What was I thinking? *You weren't, dummy.* You were just a lay. To each their own, I guess.

I decide to bypass breakfast. He seems like he'll have his hands full. Walking out of his house and across the way, I unlock the door to my tiny shoebox of a home and slam it shut. What a prick. I wasn't into him anyway. A dick is just a dick—

I jump at the sudden intrusion of my front door opening and turn to see Trevor barreling through. "Jesus, knock much?" I walk away, heading toward the kitchen.

"Why'd you leave?"

"Uh, seriously?"

"Yeah, seriously." He's right behind me.

"Dude, your gang bang arrived. Sorry if I gave you the wrong impression last night, but I'm not into that kinda shit."

He stops me by grabbing my shoulder. "What the fuck are you talking about?"

"Trevor, it's cool. I get it. We're just fucking. Nothing else. I don't care what else or who else you screw, but I'm not into orgies." *I don't think.* He looks confused. "The two women who came over? Bimbo Barbie and her little skipper?"

"*Darlene?*"

He even says her name like it's no big deal. God, I'm so stupid. "Sure. But for real, I have stuff to do today. Burial for Herald...or Bill. So, if you don't mind—"

"Lucy, Darlene's my ex-wife."

Oh, this is news. "You were married?" Maybe something he could have mentioned.

"Was. Keyword."

Great, so he's banging his ex. Doesn't help him any.

"Okay, well...great. Anything else?"

"Yeah, the other one is her girlfriend."

Wait. Step back. "Girlfriend?"

"Yeah, as in lover. She's a fucking dyke. Loves pussy now. Hence why we're divorced."

Gotta admit, I didn't see *that* one coming. "Are you still—"

"Hung up on her? Fuck no. We've been divorced for five years now. And our marriage was done before that. She comes over with Kiki to use the beach. And I guess now is a good time to tell you we have a kid together." *Jesus!* "Is that a problem for you?"

"So, you're not having a gang bang with your ex and her lesbian lover?"

"Fuck no."

"And you have a kid."

"Yes."

Not what I was expecting to hear. I mean, how's that gotta feel being left for a chick? Ouch. And the kid thing? It shouldn't shock me. He is old enough to have a child.

And does it bother me? I guess not. As long as I don't have to be its mommy. "No. I don't see that as a problem."

"Good. Anything else you want to hash out or ask me?"

Possibly who the woman was the other day. But that makes me seem like some jealous girlfriend. And I'm far from that. "Nope. All good."

He grabs me by the waist, pulling me into him. "Good. Now, about breakfast."

———

"Did you want to say a few words?" he asks, that sexy smile on his face.

I look away and down at the burial site. "You two were great lobsters. You brought so much joy to the world. You will be greatly missed." Yeah, I said two. Poor Bill/Herald kicked it while I was gone. As Trevor took the two lobsters and dug a hole in the back of Gran's house, I decided I wasn't one to own pets.

Trevor places a kiss to the top of my head, no doubt

laughing at me, and grabs my hand. "Now, let me get some food in you. I plan on working you really hard today. Gonna need those nutrients."

Trevor takes the day off, and I feel pretty special since he admits it's the first time he's taken a day to himself since he's opened the doors to Four Fathers. I want to high five myself for being so amazing, someone would break a pretty solid record of most consecutive days at work for me. I won't deny I'm sure my excellent skills in the bedroom, kitchen, beach...uh, shed, have a thing or two to do with it, though.

Since I decline going back to his place to make a family breakfast with his ex, he suggests a small breakfast joint down the shore. The sun's out and there's barely a cloud in the sky. Trevor opted for no shoes, so I follow suit. He's quiet on the walk over, but I'm totally cool with the silence. He's lost himself in the peacefulness of the ocean, and I can see how. The sound of the waves is calming. We're walking close enough, our bodies brush against one another. It feels intimate in a way, but then again, I could just be over analyzing it. But there's no doubt his hand purposely grazes mine every few steps.

I stare off ahead, the brightness of the sun causing me to squint, when the guy from the other day comes into view. "Hey, I know that guy."

"Who?" Trevor asks, looking ahead as my new friend approaches.

"I knew I recognized you," I say, smiling at the guy I met at the seafood shop. "Jax, right?"

"That's right. Good memory, Lucy." Jax turns to Trevor. "Trevor."

"Jax," Trevor replies.

I quickly glance at Trevor, who's lost his easy-going smile. "Wait, you two know each other?" I ask, shocked.

"Jax Wheeler is Eric's neighbor," he answers, not taking his eyes off Jax. I'm feeling a bit of a cock fight coming on, and it's not because I'm all hot and fight worthy. It's because Trevor reaches out and grabs my hand.

Well, if *that's* not making a statement.

"What brings you out here? Bit out of the way for you," Trevor asks, pulling me into him. I can't help but smile at his clear attempt at claiming his territory. I look at Jax, awaiting his response, but he doesn't look in a hurry to answer him. He's staring, with that killer smile aimed directly at me. I'd be lying if I didn't admit a small amount of heat swirls in my belly. He's not nearly as hot as Trevor, but that smile? Yikes. A girl could find herself in trouble with him.

"Just enjoying the views." Again, his eyes never leave mine.

The grip Trevor has on me tightens. As much as I'm enjoying this, the need to get this show on the road is more important. I'm hungry. For my man and some eggs benedict.

"Okay, well. Great running into you again. Trevor promised to fill me up on yummy food, amongst other things, so...we better get going."

Jax's smile doesn't falter, but his eyes say otherwise. Trevor seems to be done with the small talk. He pulls me along, and I glance behind me, waving at Jax as a last-ditch effort to be polite.

"That wasn't very—"

Startling me, he picks me up and throws me over his shoulder. "I'm gonna fill you up, huh? Other things in mind besides breakfast?"

I start to laugh and squeal as his hand smacks across my butt cheek. "Nope, just breakfast. Sausage. Love me some big sausage lin—"

He smacks me again. "I'm pretty sure we don't need to go to breakfast to get a sausage in your mouth." He starts to turn around, and I laugh while trying to hang on upside down over his back.

"No! I need food. Real food. The sausage that's not frowned upon when you bite it." The sound of his own laughter does something to me. A slow burn that blows away heat brought on earlier by Jax. My stomach takes that opportunity to growl.

Still groping my butt, his voice deep with humor, amongst other things, he says, "Well then, let's get some sausage in you."

God, I've never craved sausage so much in my life.

━━━━━

Breakfast turns out to be amazing. Trevor orders an omelet and I get the eggs benedict. We share a plate of pancakes, and of course, he orders three large sides of sausage links. We eat them all, and I mess with him the entire time by putting them in my mouth and sucking. He tries taking me into the bathroom, threatening to put his dick in my mouth as a lesson, but the bathroom is out of order. We both kinda lost on that one.

After I'm stuffed to the hilt, Trevor takes me surfing. I'm super scared since I'm not a fan of the water, so he takes me into the equipment shed and fucks the nerves right out of me. Then he gets me on a board. And I surf! It was fucking awesome! We have lunch on the beach, and dinner around a bonfire at his place. The sun sets, and still, we chat about nothing, just enjoying one another.

I tell him how I used to work at a middle school in the music program before I came here, and how much I really enjoyed it. That's when he tells me about his son, Kaden, who is almost twenty-one and in college. If he is anything like his dad, I'm sure he's a great guy.

The night turns into another day of sightseeing, eating, and screwing like animals. Our days blend into one another until three pass. Trevor starts having not a single care in the world. He's content and playful. And I really like that about him. He isn't counting so much, which I maybe have something to do with, and he's sleeping. He said before me, sleep wasn't an easy task for him. We go four whole days just being in our own little bubble, until I start to see the stress back on his face. He receives numerous calls from work, which he excuses himself to take, and when he returns, he's counting under his breath without acknowledging it. I call him out in the beginning, but notice it stresses him out more, so I stop.

On day five, he tells me he has to go into work for a bit and we'll meet up later. I'm super bummed. I've been enjoying our days together, but hope maybe going into work and dealing with whatever he is avoiding will take some pressure off him.

I get the feeling his partner is a major prick. From the voicemails I can vaguely hear, he sounds super demanding. Like a boss more than a partner. It makes me instantly not like him, but Trevor vouches he's a solid guy, so whatever.

Either way, I play it cool, saying no big deal, and allow him to walk me to my door before he leaves for work. Maybe I can use the day to search for a part time job to ensure I won't starve for the remainder of the summer.

The only ringer is, when I step out onto my front porch to walk into town, Trevor's car is still parked in his driveway. And oddly more, I catch a glimpse of a woman entering his house.

EIGHT

TREVOR

THE PROBABILITY OF HER, A RANDOM VARIABLE, relocating and taking this job, the measurable subset of the negative effect due to insufficient constrained—

"Stop," I scold myself. "Fucking stop." I walk through the hallway of Rumson Middle School after meeting with an old friend who teaches there and is currently holding summer classes for the music program.

Even with Dr. Winter's session today, the stress is building. Eric's on my ass. He wants me in the office. The warehouse project is in full effect, and he wants reassurance the numbers are where they need to be. Highest return. I've never been wrong. I've also never been one to blow him off. I know that eats at him. Smug bastard thinks everyone should bow to him. He may have helped save me, but he isn't my boss. I don't answer to him, or anyone.

Invertibility of the equation admits, at most, a countable number of roots—

"Dammit, stop!" I slam my hands to my temples and start to count down from ten, trying to reroute my thoughts. The last few days have been amazing. Ever since Lucy, things have been...different. The counting has all but stopped. I've found sleep. I've laughed. I've fucked more than I have in ages. It's as if she's saving me. From what? Probably myself. The negative factor in it all is once the summer comes to an end, we'll close on her Gran's house and she'll leave. I can't let that happen.

I did some quick research after Lucy told me how much she enjoyed her old job. Cheryl, now a music teacher, owed me a favor. Hopefully, it will pay off and I can convince Lucy to stay—no, force her to. She's not leaving.

I canned the tear-down of her Gran's house. I still plan on purchasing the lot, so Lucy can have the money from it, but the house is hers. The stories she tells, how happy she looks, her voice is like music to my ears—a silencer to the madness inside my head. I couldn't take that away from either of us. So, I'm going to call off the dogs. I'm willing to do anything to keep her in my life— keep the sanity she brings to it. Once I get the application, I'm forcing her to take the job. There's no other solution.

My phone vibrates again in my pocket. Eric's been blowing it up the last hour.

I need to get to work. I need to get my shit done and get back to Lucy.

"You wanna look at your watch again or finish this shit up?" Eric snaps at me. Don't know why he even fucking cares. The meeting is done. All the partners are sitting around spilling bullshit about who they're sticking their dicks into. My purpose for being here is done. I need to get back home. "Clearly you have more important things to be doing. Feel free to share with us who has your attention lately." His tone is laced with annoyance.

The stress returns full blast, and the numbers start piling. I slide my hands over my face and tug at my hair, needing my head to stay clear. "First off, none of your business. Second off, yep, none of your business."

Mateo slaps his hand on the table, bursting out laughing. "Whoa there, cowboy. Want to tell us something? You got a girl keeping your dick warm finally?" I'm irritated that he puts Lucy in a category of just being a lay for me.

"You're telling us you found someone who puts up with you and those stupid ass sandals you always wear?" Levi chimes in.

I'm done with this. I stand, tossing the folder holding today's numbers at Eric. "Numbers are solid. I'll be remote the rest of the week if you need me." I walk off, letting those assholes laugh at my expense.

I'm out of the conference room when Eric grabs me. "Wait just a second."

I turn, waiting for the undermining. "What?"

"What? How about where the fuck have you been all week?"

I brush his hand off me. "Handling some shit. None of your business."

"It is when you blow off the company. You sat through half that shit mumbling. You slipping again?"

My hands begin to shake as I fight the tornado in my head. The personal file I'm holding slips out of my grip and falls to the ground. Eric is down before me, gathering the strewn papers and picking up one in particular.

"What's this?" He waves the application for the teaching position.

"Nothing." But there's no hiding the stress on my face. I don't need his scrutiny right now. "Listen, I'm fine. Just leave it alone."

"The hell you are. I know when you're not fine. What's got your head all jammed? Whatever it is, *whoever* it is, get rid of her. It's not helping you or this business." I take in his cold, calculating stare a second longer before snatching the contract out of his hands and shoving it inside the pocket of my suit coat. Turning my back, I walk away before I take my fist to his perfectly manicured face. He knows nothing about happiness. He hasn't truly been happy since Julia, who took off on him several years ago.

"Where the fuck you going? Don't walk away from me, Trevor."

I don't bother turning around as I address him. "I'm going to live my life the way I want to." And then, I'm gone.

By the time I pull into my driveway, I'm a fucking wreck. I'm reciting the exact measurements of my driveway as I pull in, counting down the exact second until I park. The three Xanax I popped are doing shit for me.

I barely shut my car off before jumping out and heading across the way.

NINE

L U C Y

THE FIRST THING I'M GONNA DO WHEN I WIN THE lottery is hire someone to do my laundry. I mean, how much detergent goes into this shit? I hear the door open and assume it's Trevor. That or someone else feels comfortable walking in Gran's house. *Do ax-murderers knock?* Seeing Trever storm down the hallway, I feel a bit relieved.

I live to see another day.

"Look who the cat dragged—*whoa!*"

He's behind me, trapping my body between him and the dryer.

"I need to fuck you."

Oookay then. He thrusts against me, and I throw my hands onto the dryer for support. His hands wrap around my yoga pants, tugging at them. My tummy starts to swirl with excitement. I'm all for hot, spontaneous sex, so I allow him to undress me—more like tear my clothes off.

"Hey, don't tear the goods, I only have two pairs," I joke.

He has my pants down, jerking at my underwear. "I'll buy you more."

I love sex with Trevor. He's going to destroy sex with any future guy for me. Because let's face it, his dick is top notch. But something seems off with him. I'm quickly learning his moods. He's mumbling, which I'm sure he doesn't realize, spitting out equations that would put Einstein to shame—a sign I know he's trying to compress something.

He tears my panties down, then pulls one hand away to release himself from his pants, aligns himself, and with two hands back around my hips, he slams inside. "Oh shit," I moan. He feels so much bigger from behind. My legs almost buckle, but he holds me up, pulling out and slamming back in. My grip tightens on the dryer, holding myself in place, but it's impossible. He's on a mission.

"I need all of you right now," he grunts, fucking me like a madman. In and out, he pounds into me. He's so deep. Maybe it's the position, or the valiant effort he's making, but it's as if he's willing to break me just to get even deeper.

This isn't like our normal sex. It's more aggressive. Not that I'm complaining. I'm about to have an orgasm that's surely gonna blind me. I moan, and cuss, begging for him to fuck me harder. And he does. *Fuck, fuck, fuck, I'm going to come. Fuck, I'm going to come...* "Fuck, Trevor, I'm *coooooming...*" I almost bite my tongue off. My walls squeeze down so tight, I may have cut off the circulation to his dick. He's nearing his climax too. Trevor takes complete control slamming my ass into him, fucking me, one, two, and on the third thrust, I feel him buckle. The growl...*God*, it's so hot as he orgasms.

I try to catch my breath as I fall onto the dryer, thankful for the flat surface. It was that or tumbling face-first to the ground. Trevor breathes heavily behind me, no doubt trying to talk his heart out of evicting itself from his chest.

"I think we just moved the dryer five feet forward," I sigh.

He doesn't respond.

I lift my head to look back, making sure he's still alive. What just happened would kill a lesser man. "Hey, you still with me?" He still doesn't speak, but presses his lips to my shoulder, kissing behind my ear, my neck. I'm now positive something's up. I just don't know if it's safe to ask. At least he stopped counting.

I wish I could help ease his mind, give him some relief from all the commotion in his head. A part of me feels like what just happened was his way of getting that. Kind of a win-win for us both. But over the past couple days, he's become more than just a neighborly hook up for me. And as much as I want to deny it, the gooey feels are starting to build.

"Man, tacos sound good right now, don't they?

Guacamole, ground beef, chips. Lots of chips."

He squeezes me and chuckles in my ear. "I love tacos."

———

We're on the back deck, Trevor sitting on the lawn chair, me curled up in his lap. We just got done devouring a mound of tacos and I'm trying not to barf at how full I am. Trevor's mood has changed. We got cleaned up and walked down to the local grocery mart for supplies to make tacos. He grabbed a billion more things like cereal, lunch meat, and every day stuff that would taste *horrible* in tacos, then insisted on paying the bill. Now, with a full fridge and a fuller belly, we're quietly enjoying the evening sounds of the ocean.

"Hey, Trev?"

"Yeah," he responds, kissing the top of my head.

"What's with the sandals?" He sighs. "I mean, it's hot. You seem to pull off anything, but I never see you in dress shoes."

He presses another kiss to my head. "From the age of

twelve to eighteen, I lived on the streets. As I said before, my mother hated me. She saw me as a freak, so she took me to the beach one day and left me there. The only things I had were the clothes on my back. When she left, she didn't even make sure I had shoes on." Jesus, what a bitch. "I spent years on the beach. Living off things tourists would forget and leave behind. I barely ever wore shoes. But it was freeing for me. I got so used to always feeling the sand beneath my toes. Being that way for so long, once I was able to afford the finest pair of shoes, I hated it. It stressed me out. My counting would get worse. I became agitated anytime I had to enclose my feet. Sandals allow me to feel free. It's what works since walking barefoot into work isn't an option."

I pull away and turn so I can get a good look at him. "I'm sorry that was your life."

He tucks my hair behind my ear. "Don't be. It's in the past." I want to argue and call his bluff. The way he suffers is very much in the present. He fights this battle daily. I see it. I watch him struggle. I want to say I've helped take his mind away from the madness, but it's still there.

"Why the sad face?"

"I just feel horrible that someone would do that to such a wonderful person. I don't know how you go through what you do. I can barely count the fingers on both of my hands. But I think you're pretty darn great. And I kinda like you, so I just want happiness for you."

God, that sounded cheesy—

His lips claim mine and he kisses me. Like *kissses* me. His hands are around my face, pulling me into him, his lips devouring mine. It's not our norm of mauling at each other. It's slow. He opens my mouth with his tongue, and I invite him inside, allowing them to dance around one another. He doesn't take the kiss any farther, but he's giving me more than what the rest of our bodies could offer. I think, which is just a guess, he's telling me he kinda likes me too.

NINE

L U C Y

"NEVER!" I SCREAM, MY HEART BEATING OUT OF my chest. I run for dear life, knowing he's super close behind me.

"Take it back or I'm gonna spank that ass until you're begging me to stop." He also sounds out of breath.

I run the rest of the way up the beach to his house and take the stairs two at a time. *Go, go, go,* I chant, making it to the deck and throwing open the sliding glass door. "I saw it! Can't be mad at me!" I partially yell, partially laugh, making my way through the ginormous kitchen when his arm reaches out and snatches me. I'm over his shoulder and his free hand kneads my ass cheek. I scream at the top of my lungs, giggling. I'm in big trouble, and don't know whether to be nervous or thrilled.

"Take it back. Or I'm gonna push you down to your knees and shove my cock in your mouth until you do."
Jesus, give me something worth being afraid of. I squirm in his hold.

"Guess you're gonna have to get me on my knees," I say, and he chuckles.

He flips me back, placing my feet back on the ground. "Down you go." His eyes are daring. Mine are challenging. A few seconds pass, then I'm getting on my knees. My pussy clenches at the way his eyes become dark. He's already hard as a rock. His hand disappears into his board shorts and he pulls out his dick. "Open that sweet mouth of yours," he says, his voice dark. God, I'm gonna come just by the way he's talking to me. Gone is the playfulness, and in its place is the man in charge.

I do as I'm told. He takes a step closer and puts the tip of his dick on my bottom lip. I've never been so excited for anything in my life and fight not to touch myself. I stick out my tongue and lick his tip. He groans, pushing farther into my mouth.

"Be a good girl and suck me," he demands, bringing a hand behind my head and pushing me into him. I'm so turned on. Hot with need. I open wide and work him into my mouth. His hips stroke in and out and with each drag of my tongue he moans. He's so big, I do my best to loosen my throat. I want to take as much of him as I can. I lift my hand and cup his balls, massaging them while my other hand wraps around, squeezing his tight ass.

"Fuck," he groans louder, pulling at my hair. He works his hips faster, causing a few gagging close calls on my end. I work him hard and fast, sucking deep on his tip and stroking his shaft. "Fuck, babe," he moans, using both hands to force my head forward and back. I'm bobbing, sucking, fucking his dick with my mouth. I'm wet as hell, dying for my own release. His cock swells even more, his balls tighten in my hold, and without pulling away, he comes down my throat.

Once I suck him clean, he pulls out, tucking himself back in his pants. "Now, if you take it back, I'll eat your pussy until you come all over my tongue."

"I take it back. I didn't see a grey hair," I say without a second thought.

———

I throw my tank top over my head and shimmy into my shorts. "Hey, I'm gonna run home and get some fresh clothes," I yell to Trevor, who's still in the shower.

"No, wear something of mine."

I chuckle. "No, I need real underwear."

"Don't you fucking dare put underwear on. I'll just rip them off you." And goddammit, he will. I'm down to three pairs since he's demolished every other. I'm almost to the point where I'm gonna have to start sewing the threads back together and re-wear them.

"I promise I won't be long." I know he doesn't want me to leave. He's made that known. Aside from the meetings he's had to adhere to three times a week, we've been together. It's been a solid month of complete madness. Awesome madness. And it's not just the bomb ass sex. That alone is worth never leaving his side. But

Trevor Blackstone is amazing. He's kind, funny, attentive. From the times I've seen him talk with his son, he's a great dad. I actually got to meet Darlene, and minus knowing their history, she's a hoot. There's still that platonic love for each other, even though Trevor always acts extremely annoyed with her. Kiki is great too. Closer to my age, so we have a lot in common, minus the large fake boobs and professional dancing skills. But there have been times when Trevor's had to run off to handle work stuff, leaving Kiki and I to swap music recommendations.

Every day I spend with Trevor, I fall a little bit harder. It's kinda hard not to. He's a great guy who thinks life revolves around me. I mean, who wouldn't enjoy that? He says things. Coded words. If I sat down and dissected them, they would probably have some big meaning behind them. But he never pushes, and I don't want to guess that it means something it doesn't. At any moment, he could take back all the free lunchmeat in my fridge and decide never to talk to me again.

But I'm a smart girl.

I know whatever is going on between us is real. Growing. A bit confusing, because I don't think I've ever felt so deeply for someone in my life. Well, aside from my parents and grandparents. But after thinking long and hard about it, I think I am. I'm that four-letter word, in love. The flutters twirl in my belly at how insane that sounds. He's close to twenty years older than me. Is age a factor? To be honest, no. But should it be? I won't lie, it worries me. What if he gets bored? What if someone more his age comes around and woos him? Someone more mature? Because I'm seriously lacking a lot of that in my life.

I also have to factor in that I'm only here a few more weeks. Once the summer's over, I have to sell the house. It's gonna kill me to see Gran's place be demolished, but without that money, I'm dead broke. Well, I'll still be dead broke. What I'll make will barely cover the first and second mortgages and back taxes she wasn't paying, but hopefully it should be enough for a plane ticket back home and a ride to the government office to register for food stamps.

The point is, I leave soon.

Unless he asks me to stay.

Come on, Lucy. He's not going to ask.

That pessimistic side of me agrees. I've thrown out some hints about the summer ending and Trevor shuts them down every time. He gets agitated and changes topics. He blames his change in mood on work. But I'm not sure what to believe.

"I have something I want to show you, so don't take too long. Then again, I'm aching to find a reason to take my palm to that sweet ass of yours." I smile and wiggle my butt at him. I flash him my tits for good measure, and I'm on my way. I'm already trying to picture my pile of clean clothes so I know what to grab and head right back. My fingers wrap around the doorknob just as it opens, pushing me back.

"Whoa!" I catch myself as a man walks in, acting like he owns the place. "Excuse me, can I help you?"

He stares down at me, giving me the creeps. "Can

you help me? The question is who the fuck are _you_?"

Dude, what a prick! "I'm Lucy, the neighbor, and you?"

His smile fills his features, but it's nothing like Trevor's. His is cold. Cruel, almost. "Ahhh, the neighbor. I assume you're the cause of his distraction."

"Distraction?"

"Trevor's a smart man. A busy man. He's needed. He doesn't have time to be playing around with a little poor, stubborn girl just to close on a house faster."

His insult cuts deep, just like he wanted. I wish I didn't show how it affected me, but his evil smirk tells me he knows it did. "He's not...you don't know anything about me...or us," I snarl back at him.

"I don't? You aren't the golden ticket to him tearing down that piece of shit, eye-sore next door? I commend my friend for getting in your pants to trick you into selling sooner. Our business needs his full attention, though. Do us all a favor. Sell the goddamn house already and go back to your playground, wherever that is. He's too old to play games with you."

He brushes off his suitcoat, as if I've dirtied it. "Oh, do tell me you know about the contract? The one he carries around, waiting for the right time to force it on you?" He starts to laugh. "He was right when he said you were a dumb little nitwit."

"I don't believe you. He wouldn't say that."

"Not my problem. Just do us both a favor and sign so you can get out of his hair." He doesn't give me another second of his time. He walks out of the house and into his fancy car.

I stand there, stone still as he pulls away. He's lying. Trevor feels something for me. If I were just a conquest to get that contract signed, I'd know it. Wouldn't I?

Oh God. Has this all been a farce? I recall the first time he came to my door, demanding I sign the new contract, but he never asked again. Was it because he had a plan? Was *this* his plan?

I feel sick to my stomach. Is that what he was going to show me? I turn, heading back to his room. I'm quiet in hopes he doesn't realize I've returned. I go into his closet and sift through his coat jackets. Which one did he have on? Dammit, they all look the same. I start feeling at the pockets until I hit pay dirt. Digging into the coat pocket, I pull out a folded paper. *No.* My heart plummets. It's the new contract. Everything is complete, save for the date and my signature.

Whoever that man was, he was telling the truth. My assumptions tell me I just met his jerk off business partner.

Fuck me. And fuck him.

How stupid can I be? I wipe a tear off my cheek and shove the paperwork back in his pocket. I leave Trevor's and make my way back to Gran's. I storm into the house, but stop in my tracks. When I look around, I don't see just my Gran's house anymore. I see memories of him. Images of the past month he's made so wonderful for me. Us on the couch, him touching me so gently, as if I would break in his arms, to images of him losing complete control and pushing me so far into oblivion with his mouth, his hands, his words, it threatened to shatter in a million glorious pieces.

But it was all a sham.

And I'm the dumb girl who fell for it.

I rip my eyes away from anything reminding me of him and hurry down the hallway. "Maybe he's right. I am just a dimwit. Falling for someone who was too good to be true. God!" I yell, wanting to throw myself on the bed and cry for being so naïve. But that bed is another reminder of the bad choices I make.

I can't stay here anymore. "I'm sorry, Gran, I can't do this anymore." I swipe at my soaked cheeks and grab a few things while I order an Uber. I'm in such a hurry, I forget to grab the letter Gran gave me. On the car ride, I deplete the remainder of my savings for a plane ticket home.

TEN

TREVOR

I LOOK AT THE CLOCK BEFORE THROWING A SHIRT over my head. *What the fuck's taking her so long?* The itch I get anytime she's not in my presence quickly returns. I can't imagine her leaving at the end of the summer. That's why tonight, I'm going to change that. With the music job application now in hand, it's time to force my girl to stay.

My mind takes me back to earlier this morning watching her sleep. It sounds creepy as fuck, but God, how beautiful she looked in my arms. She's like an angel bringing me peace. It's been too long since I've enjoyed the quietness of my life. When she's not around, my head explodes and the numbers become louder. More cluttered. Almost too much to handle. It's fucking maddening.

Dr. Winters thinks I should go in for an evaluation. But I don't need therapy. I need *her*. I need to be with her. In her. Tasting her. Fucking her. Owning her. There's not a time where I'm not thinking about fucking her so far into submission, she knows who she belongs to. But there's that part of her that doesn't require it. She knows who owns her. I fucking do.

I walk over to the front door and step outside as a car pulls away. Barefoot, I walk next door, ready to drag her back, dressed or not. She doesn't need clothes. I'll buy her anything she wants. The whole goddamn department store.

I twist the knob to walk in, but it's locked. *What the fuck?* I bang on the door. "Luce, open up." I give it a few seconds, then jiggle the knob again. "Lucy! Seriously, get out here, or I'm gonna take your ass with my cock." I laugh for a second, trying to mask my anxiousness. I start banging harder, frantic. "Open the fucking door!"

Silence.

I take off behind the house and run three stairs at a time up to her back deck. I pull at the sliding glass door, but it's locked too. I look inside and don't see movement. I look through each window I can reach, but the rooms are absent.

"What the fuck?" I reach for my phone to call her when I realize I don't even know her number. She's never been out of my sight long enough to have to call her. Panic seizes me. I dial Clara's number, but get her voicemail.

"Trevor Blackstone. I need the contact information for Lucy. The granddaughter for the Flanders Bay property. Call me back ASAP."

I hang up. Where the fuck could she have gone? The thought of her possibly injured sends me into a whirlwind. *Numbers, probabilities, ratios...* There's no way she would not be answering me. Images of her lying inside hurt or even worse... I don't think, I act. Picking up the lawn chair, I toss it into the sliding glass door, shattering the glass. I call out her name again as I power through the house.

Nothing.

I search everywhere. But she's not here. I break down everything I see and create a probable solution. Her belongings are gone. The dresser is cleared of her minimal things. When I race into the bathroom, I find it cleared out.

Everything's gone.

Including her.

The vase with orange crossandra's I brought her, once resting beautifully on her bookshelf, now lays on the floor in ruins.

Then I remember the car.

Why the fuck would she leave?

My mind begins to break. She wouldn't leave me. We were good. She knew the solace she was providing. The way she brought so much peace to my life. I was going to give her everything. I thought we wanted the same things.

She wouldn't leave. She wouldn't.

I'm so clouded with confusion as the theories take

over. The pain, a stabbing realization causes my chest to constrict. It's been a lifetime since my mother's dark words rose to the forefront of my memory, but it all comes crashing down.

You're a retard boy—a freak show. Look at you with all that babbling. How do you expect me to love you? Anyone to love you? No one will stick around once they learn what you are. You're better off dead.

Picking up the nearest object, I throw it across the room, the thoughts becoming too consuming to control. I grab something else. Then another, then another. I destroy everything in sight until there's nothing but destruction surrounding me. Blood flows over my palms and between my fingers, cuts from wood, glass. The pain doesn't register because my brain is so loud, it's deafening.

Every emotion wrenches my entire being, but betrayal stands out the most.

I should have never let my guard down. I should have never allowed her in.

ELEVEN ——————

T R E V O R

Two weeks later

WALK INTO FOUR FATHERS, PRIMED IN MY NAVY SUIT holding the financial file for the warehouse deal. Everything is set for the start of the sale today. "Who's in?" I ask the receptionist.

"Morning, Mr. Blackstone. Everyone's here. Just waiting on the seller. Conference room is all set up." I nod, walking away.

"Look who decided to grace us with his presence," Eric says as I walk past him. He's wearing a cocky ass smirk on his face. "Care to explain where you've been?"

"No," I reply, walking into my office. Dropping the folder, I remove my suit jacket and hang it on the coat rack.

"Has to be something—or *someone*—keeping you away and forgetting your responsibilities to this company."

It's been me hitting rock bottom and relapsing. Two weeks of long nights running, even longer days pacing, destroying my mind with thoughts, reasonings. Not enough sessions with Dr. Winters will cure what Lucy did to me. I raise my head, giving him my full attention. "It's nothing. Not anymore. Fucking drop it."

"I won't when I feel my business is affected—"

"OUR BUSINESS. Our fucking business. I'm sick of you acting like you're the one in charge here. You may have saved my ass a long time ago, but I've more than repaid my debts to you, so fuck off. And stay the fuck out of *my* business."

Eric's eyes are a ball of fire. No one speaks to him that way. Not even me. But I'm done. The counting starts, and I know no matter how bad I fight it, I can't hide it.

"You're not focused. I'm just trying to look out for

you. You need to see Dr. Wint—"

"I *AM* SEEING HER! I SEE HER EVERY FUCKING DAY! Christ! I'm fucked up, can't you just deal with it? What I have is a curse, not a gift. A fucking curse." I slam my hands down on my desk, dropping my head.

I'm so tired of being this way. My money allows me access to any medical resources out there and nothing can be done to scrape my brain to rid me of this disease. That's what it is—what it's always been. I thought I found a cure. She was going to be my savior. I let my guard down, and she fucking tricked me. I refuse to admit how deep I felt for her. But she had me fooled. The only way I know to get past this is to allow the anger to guide me. I'm not a man who allows some little girl to pull one on me. No, I plan on showing her the same courtesy by taking away something she loves, as she did me. Any idea of stopping the sale of her Gran's house is off the table. If she thought she could lure me in with lies, then she has another thing coming to her.

Eric approaches me, placing his hand on my shoulder. "You'll get through this. Forget about her. Focus on the next two weeks and let's close this deal. Then we'll celebrate. A huge barbeque at my house. I'll have a shit ton of women ready and willing to praise you for your good work. Plus, the boys will be there. Nixon has been asking to spend some time with you."

I take a few deep breaths to reign in my anger. I shouldn't take my shit out on Eric. He has nothing to do with Lucy deceiving me. I nod, letting him know I'll be fine. My full attention is back to where it's always been: Four Fathers. Nothing else.

———

Eric's ridiculous barbeque is in full effect. And ridiculous is putting it mildly. The motherfucker has no boundaries when spending his money. Normally he grills his own burgers, but since he's trying to impress clients, he's gone all out. The Kobe burger I just ate was wrapped in a gold leaf, for crying out loud. Not to mention the Foie gras, lobster, truffles, and caviar being carted around by a full staff. The asshole has a grill that costs more than his car—just another way to let people know he's got more money than God.

It took the full two weeks to close the warehouse deal. Eric was pleased to see the numbers skyrocket. Four Fathers' stock went through the roof. The transaction more than tripled our profit margin, and that's just for the upcoming year. We have our eye on another warehouse that will completely wipe out our competition. And I have no doubt we will. Eric doesn't like anyone being better than him.

I'm standing outside by the pool swirling a fifty-year old Macallan Sherrywood scotch when Nixon, Eric's second to youngest son, approaches me. At fifteen, the kid is every bit as tall as me and damn near as thick too.

"Hey, sorry about that. I know my dad can be a prick." Just moments before, I had to break up an altercation between him and his dad. They've never seen eye to eye, and since I've always been close with Eric, Nixon has always seemed to gravitate toward me more.

"Don't worry about it. Your dad *is* a prick." We both laugh while staring out at the full pool of family and work staff.

"Hey, Uncle Trev?" he turns to me. "Can I ask you something? What's it like? Having to live with the constant chattering in your head? Does it ever stop? Get better?"

I turn to him, looking into his green eyes. Nixon is nothing like his father. He's a great kid, excelling in school. We've always shared a bond Eric and him never did, and I know Eric despises me in some way for it. I consider his question—a question that may lead to more. I have no interest in getting in the middle of that shit storm.

"I'm not sure—"

My phone vibrates in my pocket, gaining my attention. I pull it out and see Clara calling. "Give me a second, son." I take a few steps away from Nixon and answer.

"What do you have for me?"

"Mr. Blackstone, you told me to call when she returned. It seems she arrived at the house about an hour ago."

"Start the process. Everything I have set up. I want the meeting set for tomorrow morning. First thing."

"Yes, sir."

I hang up, my grip threatening to crush the device in my hand. I knew she'd come back. It was only a matter of time before she needed that money. The anger I've fought to keep at bay returns, and I welcome it. I refuse to let my still deep, lingering feelings for her cloud my judgement. The anger is the exact fuel I need to follow through with my plans. She's going to sign that contract, and I'm going to bulldoze that shit house before the ink is even dry. Right before her eyes.

Being deprived of sleep, I've pushed myself, working out night and day, swimming, running the beach— anything to keep my mind off her. At first, I convinced myself it was all a mistake. She would come back with an explanation and things would be fine. I would force her to move in with me, so I never had to be without her. We would start making serious plans. When days passed, then weeks, I knew I had to accept it. She wasn't coming back. But now she's back, and my mind is quickly filling with confusion. The fact that I will have to see her. Want to touch her. Claim her. But it's the reminder that she's not mine, nor does she want to be, that drives that hate. Revenge.

"Everything okay, Uncle Trevor?"

I walk past Nixon. "Just fine, son. Tell your dad I had to take care of some business. I'll see you around."

I leave the barbeque, a formulation of numbers exploding in my head—all possible outcomes of the look on her face once I destroy the one thing she holds dear. Just like she destroyed my heart.

———

I pull into my driveway and notice a car parked next door. I know she doesn't have a car. *Who the fuck is over there? She could be with someone. Another man—*

I shake my head and pop a mixture of Xanax and valium. I can't allow my head to fuck this up. I jump out of my car and walk over, feeling the coldness settle in my blood. I thought about how it would be to see her again. Made sure the hatred stayed at the front of my mind so I can do what needs to be done. I don't bother knocking, and wrap my hand around the doorknob, throwing the fraying door open.

"I just don't understand—"

Her words are cut off by the sound of my intrusion. She turns to face me.

"What do *you* want?" she snaps, like I'm the enemy here. Then again, I'm about to be. "Did you do this?" she asks as a boy turns the corner from the bedroom.

"It's an old house. People break into dumps like this all the time."

Her eyes light up. She's hurt. She drops a broken frame back to the ground where she found it. "I'm sure they do. So, should I assume all robberies around here are done by muscled psychopaths?" My fingers twitch, fighting not to grab her and wrap my hand around her neck at her choice of words. "What, have nothing to say? Or was this your ploy to make it easier for me to sign the *contract*? Trash the place so I'd have to come back? Coerce me some more to move up the closing?" I don't know what the fuck she's referring to, but her accusations are stirring up the rage inside me. "You know what? I'll fucking sign your contract. You can take the house. I don't care. You won. But give me back my Gran's letter." She kicks the rubble at her feet when the little shit comes to her aid.

"Luce, calm down." She takes in a deep breath, falling into his embrace. My eyes see red at the way she's letting him touch her.

"Who the fuck are you? Her new fucktoy?"

"Fuck you, Trevor!" she spits, trying to come at me, but her lover holds her back.

"Don't. He's not worth it."

I take a predatory step closer to them. "I'd be careful

of this one, son. She's a snake—"

Lucy comes at me again, but the kid pushes her to the side. "You better watch it, asshole. Why don't you go mess with someone your own age? Practically be her fucking dad—"

I swing and punch the fucking shit. He stumbles back as Lucy screams. I move to go after him when Lucy steps between us, throwing her small hands to my chest.

"Stop! Get out of here! You've done enough. You win! You fucking win! I'll sign your damn contract. Just please give me back Gran's letter."

She's crying.

My hands begin to shake.

The overdose of pills I popped does nothing as I begin reciting number after number. "Leave, Trevor. Just get out and leave me alone." She doesn't pay me another thought as she bends down to console her new boyfriend.

I brush my hands down my face, trying to get control. Two deep breaths, and I speak. "Be at Four Fathers first thing tomorrow morning for the closing. After we close, you can have your letter."

I don't wait for her to reply. Just watching the tears fall down her porcelain cheeks is enough to ruin a man. I turn and walk out.

TWELVE

L U C Y

"ON THE BRIGHT SIDE, YOU DON'T HAVE TO PAY to get rid of anything in here. Cheaper when it's all in pieces." I turn to Devin, who I know is just trying to make light of the situation. He's already sporting a pretty awesome shiner, which makes me feel worse.

"God, I'm so sorry."

"Lucy, you're not the one who hit me. Stop apologizing."

I drop another ruined frame to the ground. "I know, but I dragged you into this. What's Katie gonna say when we come home and you have a black eye? She's going to kill me."

Devin smiles, but then grunts at the pain. "My sister will understand. I'll tell her how I went up against Rocky to avenge our girl." He comes over and offers me a hug, then continues weeding through the wreckage.

I can't believe Gran's place. My heart hurts having to take in all her belongings. Her life, just in shambles. How could he do this to me? I wipe another tear off my cheek. I didn't plan on returning here. Technology nowadays allows Electronic signatures. He could have his damn signature, but it wasn't going to be at the expense of me returning. But then I got the call. Someone had broken in and vandalized Gran's house.

The two weeks I'd spent holed up on Katie's couch did nothing for my hurting heart. There were still a few weeks until summer was over, but I just wanted this to all be over with. I prayed I could get in and out without having to see him, but that wish didn't last long when he walked through the door. The sight of him caught my breath. Even being so angry at him, he made my heart stop. He was still just as gorgeous. He looked even bigger, if that were possible.

He didn't look well, though. His eyes were lacking

that shine to them. The ones I had stared into were cold. I wanted to go to him and make things better, but I had only been a ploy to him. I never meant anything. That realization allowed me to keep my distance and anger intact.

It's a shame the anger never matched the dreams I had at night of him taking me and owning me. Every night, he would come to me and ask me to stay, and I would say yes. Then he would fuck me in such an animalistic way, I would wake up sweating.

Katie told me I could stay on her couch for as long as I needed, but what I needed was to just be done with all this. Take whatever money I could get from the sale and start over. Maybe in the country where there were no beaches, or deceiving prodigies.

When Katie got stuck on a work project, her brother Devin offered to help me. If anything, just to be a shoulder to cry on while I did one of the hardest things: officially say goodbye to Gran. I couldn't believe when I took off in such a hurry I left the letter.

At least by tomorrow morning this will all be over. No doubt, he picked the early time just to spite me. He knows damn well I'm not a morning person and waking up before nine is against my made-up religion that says I should not wake before nine.

I just need to get through tomorrow.

Then it's a new start.

In the country.

Far away from the beach.

THIRTEEN————

L U C Y

I WALK INTO FOUR FATHERS, A LITTLE STAR STRUCK. This office is amazing. Top notch, to say the least. I dressed up, though I have no idea why. There was no one I wanted to impress. Or maybe give a final *eat shit, you could have had this* send off. My black fitted dress hangs just above my knees and accentuates my boobs perfectly.

Devin laughed the entire morning while watching me pace, knowing I was speaking lies when I said this was the only thing I had to wear. But it was. This or the fifteen pairs of shorts and tank tops I brought.

Beside the point.

I walk up to the front desk, but I'm greeted by no one. I ring the bell, but no one comes out. I walk a little farther into the office, and—

"You're late." I practically jump out of my panties at his voice. I turn to see him standing a short distance from me, his bulky arms crossed over his chest.

"Yeah, well, I got stuck in bed." My comment is in regard to my issues with mornings, but the fire in his eyes tell me he took that another way.

God, he looks so good. There's no doubt I still want him. Like, bad, want him. My heart wants me to just forget why he really showed interest in me and pretend I didn't figure out his plan. My vagina seconds that plan, because she really, *really* misses his cock.

But my emotional stability tells me I need to let go. I got played. Again.

I'm going to choose not to ease his mind. He can think whatever he wants. I drop the sly act and put on my game face. "Can we just get this over with? I have things to do." Like cry.

"Follow me," he instructs, then turns, walking down a long hallway, leading us into a large conference room. A woman is already sitting at the massive table. She stands, and I recognize her voice as the realtor.

"Hello, you must be Lucy."

"Hi, that's me." I reach over and shake her hand. I go to take the seat next to her, but Trevor stops me.

"No need to sit. This won't take that long."

"Seriously?" I stare him down, wanting to punch him. How can someone go from being so amazing to such a prick? "You know what, you're right. This *won't* take long. Where do I sign?" I turn away from him, addressing Clara.

"If you can just sign here on the new contract."

Bending over, I grab the pen and scribble my signature on each page of a mountain of paperwork. When I scrawl my name on the last page, I slam the pen down. "Great. Now that that's out of the way..." I stand straight, turning back to Trevor. "Where's my letter?"

"I'll hand it over once the paperwork is filed through the courthouse. I have no doubt you may pull another fast one on me. Is that even your real signature?"

My jaw drops. The nerve. "Pull a fast one on *you*? Are

you kidding me?" I'm seeing red. "You mean you using me and pretending you liked me *just* to get me to sell my grandmother's house early!" I lift my hands and push at his chest.

"Don't insult me." He steps into me, trying to scare me with his dominance, but I'm not afraid of him.

"Oh, come on. We don't need to play dumb here. Your buddy sold you out. You don't need to act like you ever cared. Just give me back my let—"

"What do you mean my *buddy* told you? Making up lies now I see?"

"Oh, I had the pleasure of meeting who I suspect to be your douchebag of a partner. The same time he told me how you were wooing me just to get the closing moved up, you asshole!" I go to push him again, but his hands wrap around my wrist.

"You're lying."

"Fuck you! I have no reason to lie." I fight against his hold, but he only squeezes tighter.

Clara tries to step in. "Um, maybe I should—"

"Clara, leave," he barks.

"No! Clara stays," I snap. "What, afraid someone might figure out what a bastard you really are?" I make another effort, tugging at my wrists, to no avail. My chest rises and falls. I may have a heart attack. All the anger that's been simmering inside is finally getting its stage time.

"Mr. Blackstone, maybe we should take a short—"

"GET OUT, CLARA! GET THE FUCK OUT!" Trevor snaps. Clara jumps out of her chair, stumbling over her own two feet as she tries to get out of the room fast enough.

"What, get rid of any witnesses when you try to strangle—"

My words are cut off as he whips me around, aggressively stepping toward me until my back presses against the wall. "I never said that to Eric."

"Bullshit. As if I would believe you now."

"I never spoke to Eric about you. He knew nothing about you."

Oh, that's even better. Guess I was nothing to brag about. Not even his best friend knew about me. It all hurts just the same. "Well, great. No need to tell anyone about the poor little *dimwit* girl you were fucking."

"Stop."

"No, I get what I was to you."

"I said stop! I never said that."

"Who's the one lying now? I got it. No need to save face with me—"

He slams his mouth onto mine, shutting me up. I'm stunned. I didn't see that one coming. I'm stone still, unsure if this is my last kiss before he kills me. "What are you doing?" I ask, kissing him back. Dammit. I can't resist his mouth.

"I'm proving to you I'm not lying." He's doing a good job of it. He kisses me hard, pushing himself into me. My knees tremble, about to buckle. He releases my wrists and grabs my ass, lifting me so my legs wrap around his waist. I should be stopping this—fighting him off and telling him I won't be made a fool. Instead, I raise my hands and thread my fingers through his thick hair.

"I don't believe you," I whisper, increasing our kiss, missing the feel of his tongue overpowering my mouth. He presses his dick into me, and I moan.

"I think you do."

Oh God, he grinds against me, hitting my special spot. "I do—I mean, I don't! Wait, stop." I remove my hands from his hair and push on his chest. "Trevor, stop."

His hesitation is clear. He growls and lets me go, my feet falling to the ground. His eyes are dark. "Why'd you leave?"

"I wasn't going to let you use me so you could get what you want." He pulls away, giving me his back. He's distraught. I hear the numbers. "Trevor." I reach for him, but he shoves my hand off. He stops at the conference table, gripping the edge and bowing his head. "Don't turn your back on—"

"Tell me what Eric said to you."

"I already told you."

"TELL ME AGAIN," he roars, shaking the entire

table.

I take a step back. "He came over when you were in the shower. He walked in and I didn't even know who he was. He said he knew who I was and went off about how you had a plan for me and to make it easier for everyone, I should sign the contract so you can stop wasting your time with me. You needed to focus on work."

There's silence in the room. Until there's not. With the strength of a bull, he takes the table and flips it. I jump back, alarmed at his aggressive behavior. "Trevor, what are you—"

"Eric wouldn't do that to me."

"Oh, so we're back to me lying? Fine, you know what—"

He turns, his eyes ablaze, his breathing heavy. His lips are moving a mile a minute, but nothing is coming out. He's counting. Bad. It kills me to see him this way. Such a strong man looking so broken.

I step up to him, chancing that he may throw me, and with both hands, I cup his face. He's so lost in his thoughts, he doesn't register me at first. I caress his cheek, and he brings his eyes to mine. "Hey, come back to me." I wait for his eyes to dilate. His lips slowly stop.

"He wouldn't hurt me like that."

I don't know how to respond to that. Because, apparently, he would. But Eric is all he's had for so long. "I know." I pull his head down so I can reach his lips. I press mine to his and keep them there until I feel his subtle surrender. I decide to change tactics. "I left because I didn't think you wanted me." A single tear runs down my cheek. "I wanted so much more, and to think you didn't... hurt."

Snapping out of his daze, he thrusts my hands away from his face and scoops me into his arms. "I thought you were playing me." He coddles me. "You were my solace. My quiet." He takes a seat in a chair, and I snuggle into the comfort of his large frame, but I can't dismiss the feel of his heart beating hard against mine. He's mumbling quietly and fast.

I can't believe someone he cares for so much would

do something so hateful to him. I feel just as angry as he does for what he caused. The past few weeks have been torture. To find out it was all lies...

"I'm going to kill him," he mumbles.

"Me too. I'll help bury the body," I say, holding myself to him.

"I'm serious." He pulls me off him and stands.

Oh shit. I wasn't. "I was just kidding. I'm probably not even fit enough to dig a hole that deep."

He bypasses my humor and picks up the phone on the floor and punches in a few numbers. "Is Eric in yet?" Getting his answer, he hangs up and turns back to me. "Go back to my place and wait there for me."

"Yeah...that doesn't sound like a good idea. Maybe I should just stay with you."

He brings his hands around my shoulders. "I need you not to be here right now. I have so much more shit to say to you, but right now, I need you to leave and wait for me at my house."

"Trev—"

"And don't fucking leave this time." He leans down, placing his lips to mine. I'm not feeling very good about this, but I do as I'm told.

I walk out of Four Fathers with a few thoughts in mind. He wasn't using me. Life may be good again. And I also may be visiting him in jail soon.

———

I've been at Trevor's for almost two hours. I've paced the entire downstairs a thousand times. Stretched just in case I do need to do some digging. Thought about all the things I was going to say to him before they carted him off in handcuffs. Debated on whether I could live the rest of my life in a foreign country where the law wouldn't find us.

When I finally hear the door open, I gun it from the back deck to see Trevor walking in and slide to a complete stop in front of him.

"*Geeeez*. I'd hate to see the other guy," I say, looking at his bruised and bloodied face. He walks up to me, pulling me into his arms. "Do we need to run?" I feel him shake his head. "Bury anyone?" A small chuckle followed by another headshake. "Will I be having to dig any holes? I've been stretching and feel a bit more confident on how much I can dig."

He pulls me away. "No. Eric is very much alive. Barely breathing, but alive."

God, that sounds good, but not so good at the same time. "What happened?"

"I made sure he knows never to meddle in my life again." He bends down to kiss me, but groans when his cut lip brushes against mine.

"I'm sorry. I know he's your partner and best friend—"

"Stop. Eric's had that coming for years. It was something that would've happened sooner or later. We hashed it out. It's done. Let's just say he's sorry." He kisses me again. When he pulls away, I get a good look at him. Once I get past the cut lip, blood around his nose, and bruise possibly forming on his cheek, I capture his eyes.

"Are you okay, though?" I ask. "Like really okay?"

He leans in, kissing me. "No."

His answer kills me.

I start to cry.

I feel such regret for jumping the gun. If I hadn't been such a brat and left without confronting him, things would have been so different. Sudden remorse fills me. "The contract. I saw it in your coat pocket all ready to be signed," I weep, wrapping my arms around him. "Oh, Trevor, that's why I believed—"

He picks me up and carries me over to the gigantic leather couch. He sits, holding me tightly in his lap. "I had it, but the night I took you to dinner, I knew I wasn't going to make you give up your Gran's house. I knew I had other plans for you."

I smile against his shoulder. "Oh yeah? And what were those?"

"Aside from fucking you senseless? Figuring out how to get you to stay." He pulls away, cupping my cheeks. "I was going to ask you to stay that day. A friend of mine has an opening in the music department at the local school. I was going to coerce you into staying. You've been the best thing that's come into my life. It's been a long time since I've felt free. And I just can't let that go. So, whatever it took. I was willing to play dirty to make that happen."

"Well shit," I say, the tears falling freely down my face. I bring my lips to his, kissing him with all my might. I don't let him go until I'm fresh out of air and my lips become numb. Also, because I'm pretty sure I made his lip worse. When our eyes are on one another, I smile. "Well, why don't you show me just how you were going to get me to stay, so I can tell you I would love to."

EPILOGUE

T R E V O R

One month later

PULLING INTO MY DRIVEWAY LIKE A MADMAN, I leave an inch between my car and the garage. A less experienced driver would have gone straight through the house. I got dragged away for a meeting out of town, which left thirty-six hours between now and the last time I saw Lucy. Getting home and inside her was the only thing on my mind.

There's instant annoyance when I see Darlene's fucking car is here. I need Lucy to be alone because I'm gonna fuck her until she can't see straight. Little minx thought she was funny sending those dirty pictures of herself knowing I couldn't have her. She may think it's funny to mess with a man like myself, but what I have in store for her, she won't be laughing. More like screaming my name and coming all over my tongue, finger, and cock. The last photo she took was a few hours ago of her in that tiny little bikini. Made me think of her ass and how I'm going to make that mine soon too.

Stepping inside the house, I'm already getting hard thinking of all the shit I'm going to do. Starting with my cock deep down her throat.

"Luce?" I call out, dropping my bag on the couch. I look at all her stuff scattered over the living room and smile. I love that my girl is feeling more at home. She moved in immediately. I didn't give her a choice. After our blow out, things progressed fast. Once I got done fucking her in every spot of my house, I told her my plans. For everything. Starting with getting rid of the punk boy she brought back with her. She soothed my jealous mind by explaining who he was. Then I launched into my plans. For the house. For us. My sweet girl cried. Then she did something I'll always treasure. She fucked me sweet. Slow. She moaned all those little sounds I fucking love.

We spent the remainder of the summer enjoying the beach and each other. Once school was back in session, she started as the assistant music coach at Rumson Middle School. The first day she was gone, I regretted getting her the job. Having her not with me was enough for me to want to call Cheryl and get her fired. But when she came home smiling ear to ear, I couldn't take that away from her. Even if I was a selfish prick, her happiness was all that mattered. I would do anything for her.

I stuck to the plan and still purchased her Gran's house. But, instead of bulldozing it and building a mansion, I told her I was leaving it alone. Knowing the house wasn't going to be torn down, I told her she had free reign on what happened to it. I no longer cared about the eye-sore it had on the rest of the neighborhood. It had so many memories, even I turned a liking to the ratty old thing. The guilt still weighed heavily on me for trashing it, and I vowed to do anything to fix the damage.

Walking back toward the kitchen, I see empty lemonade vodka bottles all over the counter and a few pairs of shorts and tank tops littering the floor. I swear, if Darlene convinced Lucy to go skinny dipping during the middle of the day again, I'm gonna have it out with her. I shake my head, preparing to throw my ex out when I hear the voices and giggling coming from the back deck.

"Oh my God, no. I'll pass," Lucy says, laughing. *Wonder what my girl's passing on.*

"Honey, trust me. A woman's tongue is *way* better than a man's. If you ever get a chance, try one out. You won't be disappointed." *Jesus Christ.* This is why I don't need my ex hanging out over here.

"D, baby, our girl doesn't want the kitty. She just got done telling us she wants to experiment in the back, not eat pussy." All three women laugh.

How drunk are these women?

"Well, girl, I know he likes being talked dirty to. Make sure you call him—"

"Ladies. Time to go," I interrupt their girl time, all

three jumping at the sound of my voice. Lucy sees me and lights up, making my chest swell every fucking time.

"You're home!" She pops up and jumps on me. I catch her, bringing her lips to mine. She tastes sweet. Her legs go around me, and I press her body tight to mine. God, I missed her. "I thought you weren't supposed to be home until late tonight," she says, pressing kiss after kiss to my lips. My girl's had a few too many.

"I was. I couldn't stay away any longer. I cut the meeting short." Her smile is like a drug.

"I don't ever remember getting a welcome home greeting like that before," Darlene interrupts.

Kiki laughs, pretending to be offended by her comment. "Hey, I've greeted you like that!"

I don't give them another second of her time. "You know the way out. Lucy's done playing for the day."

All three women burst into a fit of laughter. I'm walking Lucy back inside when Darlene shouts, "You mean she's done playing with us! Don't forget what we told you, honey!"

Lucy falls into another fit of giggles, the sound making my dick even harder. I carry her upstairs, interested in what those damn women are filling her head with now. Last time, I had to talk her down from nipple piercings because of those two headaches downstairs. She spent the morning trying to convince me by letting me fuck her tits, selling me on how hot it would be if she had barbells bouncing back and forth while I stuck my dick between them. It was hot all right. I came on her chest and had her suck me clean. Then I told her absolutely not. I loved her nipples. I didn't need that extra freaky shit.

There was that small window where I waited for her to pout after telling her no. Not my girl. She shrugged those sexy shoulders of hers and told me we should probably do that again, just to make sure she enjoyed it without barbells. So, we did. Twice over.

Everything that came out of her mouth did things to me. She was a sweet, no shit taking, spitfire. She proved that once again when Dr. Winters showed up unannounced. A few days after settling into our routine,

Dr. Winters made a surprise visit. When I invited her in to meet Lucy, my girl went off like a firecracker telling my therapist I was a taken man and to stay the fuck away. I had to laugh at her passion. Claiming her territory. Learning who Dr. Winters was, the embarrassment filled her, but damn did it make me want her even more.

"What exactly did they tell you to say, my little minx?" I ask, setting her down on the side of the bed and rotating her so her sweet ass is on show. I pull her suit bottoms down, seeing she's already wet between her thighs.

"They told me you liked being talked dirty to." I can tell she's drunk. If she weren't, I'd consider taking her in the ass right now. I smile at her reflection in the window. How flushed her cheeks are. She's very turned on.

"Oh yeah? And what kind of dirty talk did they say I liked?" I take my hand between her legs and begin teasing her clit. Her little moans tell me to screw how drunk she is and fuck her back there now. I've missed being inside her. The first go around isn't going to be slow. But I hold back, not wanting to do anything she may not be ready for. When she finally allows me back there, I'm never leaving her alone.

"They said to call you daddy while letting you fuck me in the ass." I can't help but laugh as I insert a finger into her cunt. Dammit, she's soaking wet. I'm going to have to have a talk with my ex about what she says to my girl.

"Is that so? What did you say to that?" I ask, stroking her a few more times before inserting two more fingers.

"Ahhh...I said I didn't really have daddy issues, so it wasn't something that would turn me on." God, her mouth. I pump in and out of her, listening to her whimper with pleasure. Her ass is now pushing against my hand. I love how eager she gets. "Why, did you want me to call you daddy? You could technically be him. Being forty—"

I punch four fingers into her, and she grunts in absolute pleasure. She knows what happens when she teases about our age difference. She knows she'll get punished for her runaway tongue. "You know that makes me mad when you bring that up." I pull out and push back in as far as my fingers can go.

"Oh God, yeah. Maybe you should punish me for it then, *Daddy*."

Goddammit. My cock is so hard, I could break through cement. I pull my fingers out and swipe them roughly against her perky little ass cheek. She jumps at my assault, but there's nothing sexier than the moan that falls from her lips.

"You wanna be a bad girl, don't you?" I ask, caressing the building welt. Then I smack her again.

"Oh fuck. Yes. Super naughty. Like bad, bad, bad naughty. I was going to stay out past curfew tonight too."

Jesus, I can't help but laugh. "Oh, now you've gone and done it."

"Oh boy, better punish me really good. Put me in time out and everything." She's still rubbing her ass against me. As much as I like when a woman does talk dirty, my girl may need some practice. But her randomness turns me on even more.

"All right, baby, hold on tight. Gonna fuck the bad

girl right out of you." My pants are down, and my aching cock is out and pushing inside her. I fuck my girl hard and rough, just how she loves it.

Just how I love her.

ENJOYED THIS BOOK?
MEET THE OTHER FATHERS

Four Fathers Series by bestselling authors

J.D. Hollyfield, Dani René,

K Webster, and Ker Dukey

Four genres.

Four bestselling authors.

Four different stories.

Four weeks in April.

One intense, sexy,

thrilling ride from beginning to end!

These books were designed so you can read them out of order. However, they each interconnect and would be best enjoyed by reading them all!

KINGSTON
A FOUR FATHERS STORY

She works for him.
He doesn't care.

DANI RENÉ

OTHER BOOKS IN THE
FOUR FATHERS SERIES

KINGSTON

BY DANI RENÉ

Erotic Romance

I am arrogant. Insatiable. A single father.
I desire things that would make most people blush.
Normally, I find outlets that allow me to free the sexual
beast living within and play to my heart's content.
And when my voluptuous, innocent assistant starts
starving me after a little taste, I decide I'll let my inner
animal feed—on her.
Trouble is, once I have her, I can't let her go, and that
makes things complicated.
My name is Levi Kingston.
I am a dirty, ravenous, greedy man.
People may detest my kinks, but it doesn't stop them
from wanting me.

PEARSON

A FOUR FATHERS STORY

She's too young for him.
He doesn't care.

K WEBSTER

OTHER BOOKS IN THE
FOUR FATHERS SERIES

PEARSON
BY K WEBSTER

Taboo Romance

I am selfish. Spoiled. A single father.
I do what I want because I can.
One of my four sons is dating the hot,
young little neighbor...
Too bad it won't last long.
When I want something, I take it—even if it means
taking from my son.
My name is Eric Pearson.
I am an unapologetic, egotistical, domineering man.
People may not like me, but it doesn't stop them from
wanting me.

She's not his.
He doesn't care.

WHEELER
A FOUR FATHERS STORY

KER DUKEY

OTHER BOOKS

Love Not Included Series
Life in a Rut, Love not Included
Life Next Door
My So Called Life
Life as We Know It

Standalones
Faking It
Love Broken

Paranormal/Fantasy
Sinful Instincts
Unlocking Adeline

#HotCom Series
Passing Peter Parker
Creed's Expectations
Exquisite Taste

OTHER BOOKS

ABOUT THE AUTHOR

J.D. Hollyfield is a creative designer by day and super-hero by night. When she's not cooking, event planning, or spending time with her family, she's relaxing with her nose stuck in a book. With her love for romance, and her head full of book boyfriends, she was inspired to test her creative abilities and bring her own stories to life. Living in the Midwest, she's currently at work on blowing the minds of readers, with the additions of her new books and series, along with her charm, humor and HEA's.

J.D. Hollyfield dabbles in all genres, from romantic comedy, contemporary romance, historical romance, paranormal romance, fantasy and erotica! Want to know more! Follow her on all platforms!

SOCIAL MEDIA

Keep up to date on all things J.D. Hollyfield

Twitter
Author Page
Fan Page
Instagram
Join Reader Group
Goodreads
Amazon

ACKNOWLEDGMENTS

First, and most importantly, I'd like to thank myself. It's not easy having to drink all the wine in the world and sit in front of a computer writing your heart out, drinking your liver off and crying like a buffoon because part of the job is being one with your characters. You truly are amazing and probably the prettiest person in all the land. Keep doing what you're doing.

Thanks to my husband who supports me, but also thinks I should spend less time on the computer and more time doing my own laundry.

Thanks to all my eyes and ears. Having a squad who has your back is the utmost important when creating a masterpiece. From betas, to proofers, to PA's to my dog, Jackson, who just got me when I didn't get myself, thank you. This success is not a solo mission. It comes with an entourage of awesome people who got my back. So, shout out to Amy Wiater, Ashley Cestra, , Jenny Hanson, Kristi Webster, Amber Higbie, Amy Khel, Kara Burr Orosz and anyone who I may have forgotten! I appreciate you all!

Thank you to Monica at Word Nerd Editing for helping

bring this story to where it needed to be.

Thank you to All By Design for creating my amazing cover. A cover is the first representation of a story and she nailed it.

Thank you to my awesome reader group, Club JD. All your constant support for what I do warms my heart. I appreciate all the time you take in helping my stories come to life within this community.

Thank you to Emilie and the team at InkSlinger for all your hard work in promoting this book!

And most importantly every single reader and blogger! THANK YOU for all that you do. For supporting me, reading my stories, spreading the word. It's because of you that I get to continue in this business. And for that I am forever grateful.

Cheers. This big glass of wine is for you.

NEVER MISS UPDATES!
Sign up for J.D. Hollyfield's Newsletter!
SIGN UP!